Bearing Secrets

Alaskan Tigers: Book Eight

Marissa Dobson

Published by Sunshine Press
Printed in the United States of America
ISBN-13: 978-1-939978-46-2

Dedication

To my readers who emailed me after Tigress for Two was published asking that the Brown brothers received their stories, and to see more of the twins Turi and Trey. Here they are.

Enjoy this newest adventure to Alaska and the Brown's Island.

Bearing Secrets: Alaskan Tigers

Contents

Bearing Secrets: Alaskan Tigers

Ivy Carter's life changed in a blink of an eye. An attack on the compound she considered her home destroyed those she considered family and the life she thought she had. With her brother and the Alpha of the clan missing, she's left on her own until the Alaskan Tigers come to her rescue and whisk her off to safety.

Twins Turi and Trey Brown have had their differences, but they need to put them aside because if the pattern follows they will be next to find their mate. If that isn't bad enough, their destiny is to share *one* mate. With tension and hard feelings forming a thick barrier between them, they are going to have a challenging road ahead of them.

With so much wrong between them, how will they overcome their hardships and move on? Destiny moves in mysterious ways to bring three people who need each other together, and to bring their hearts' desires to life.

Bearing Secrets: Alaskan Tigers

Chapter One

Blood and guts caked Ivy Carter's arms and face as she huddled under the debris from a house that had been blown to bits. Whatever had been ripped apart just a few feet above had sent the gore tumbling down. Her body began to shake as terror of being discovered knotted inside her, and fearful images of what was happening raced through her mind. She didn't want to die, not like this. Death was supposed to happen when she was old and had lived a full life, not when she was still young and at the hands of those who couldn't see the bigger picture for the shifter population. Their idea of a perfect shifter world was killing those who could bring harmony to a shifter-human world; instead, they preferred to live in the shadows.

She trembled as she heard the sounds of her clan members being killed one by one. If they were mowed down so easily, there was no way her human body stood a chance. To survive she'd have to stay hidden and hope for the best. Through the crack in the debris above her, she scanned the landscape, quickly searching each of the rubble piles for any sign of life before moving on to the next. She examined the burning piles and what was left of the houses that took the brunt of the explosion knowing that even a shifter wouldn't be able to survive fire for long. Occasionally she caught a glimpse of someone fighting or alive, but none of them were the one person she searched for—her brother.

Where are you, Chad?

As the Captain of the Guards for the Alpha—Mason—he was out there somewhere, protecting him. Her stomach churned with the very thought.

Please, let Chad be safe. The first target would have been the Elders and their guards. If they hadn't found safety, none of the Elders had any chance for survival.

A deafening *boom* to her right shook the ground. The wreckage of what once was the Arizona Tigers' compound landed all around, forcing her lower into the rubble. Looking in the direction of the sound, all she could see was fire. People ran, trying to get away, but it was no use. The enemies were on their tails, tackling them to the ground and tearing out their throats before they had a chance to cry out. One by one, her clan died at the mercy of the rogues, and she could do nothing but watch.

Adjusting to get a better view of what was happening without revealing herself, she pressed her hand against the dirt wall, and pain shot through her arm. She glanced down and for the first time realized how badly she was injured. Blood poured from the jagged cut across her forearm, and glass stuck out of her flesh as though it had grown there. Pulling the shard from her skin, she watched the crimson well up in the gash then spill over until it ran like a river down her arm. It could have been much worse.

Only because she'd been in the basement doing laundry had her life been saved when the rocket exploded into the house she'd shared with her brother. Had the rogues known Chad lived here? Could that have been why her home was one of the first to be targeted? A plan to eliminate the Captain of the Guards first, then with no protection Mason would be an easier kill.

Keep it together. This is no time for me to lose it. She ripped a piece of her shirt off to make into a tourniquet and tied the fabric around her arm the best she could with her left hand. Black spots filled her vision and the world began to swirl. She wasn't sure if it was from loss of blood, terror, or a combination, but the timing couldn't have been worse. If she let unconsciousness claim her she'd be at the mercy of the rogues and she couldn't let that happen if she wanted to survive.

Footsteps crept closer, crunching glass under their weight. Not wanting to be caught, she slipped down onto the ledge. With her eyes closed, she held her breath to prevent herself from crying out. A shifter's sense of smell was greater than anything else; she only hoped since they were there to destroy the clan they'd bypass her. *If* her fear didn't give away her position before he could move past her little hiding spot. Shifters loved to put terror in their victims, and that alone could make her a whole new target.

"Randolph, the clan's been eliminated. The team will be heading back shortly." There was a brief pause and she realized the person walking past her hiding spot was on the phone. "We'll be ready to move on the next clan in a few days. Give the men a few days off, and let the other clans think this was a fluke instead of an assassination of Mason and his members for their agreement."

Assassination. Anger poured through every cell of her body. This clan was her family. They had taken her in when no one else would, and not one of them held her past against her. *Until today.* Now that they had apparently all been killed, she cast a glance about, seeking something she could use to kill. The only weapon she had was the gun, and she'd emptied the last bullet into the man who blew up the house. Her fury would have to wait unless she wanted to get herself killed.

She forced a series of shallow breaths into her lungs, trying to calm herself as he continued past her. When she could no longer hear him, she rested her head against something hard, but she didn't have the strength to move. *Just five minutes to make sure they're really gone, then I'll move.* She had to find a way out and get help before someone else suffered as her clan had.

Chad, where are you? She let her eyes drift shut, allowing the glorious darkness claim her.

* * *

A deep voice hollering from above pulled her back from oblivion, sending her pulse racing until it was thrashing in her ears. It took her a moment to realize where she was and the memories of what had happened flooded back.

Chad? Was he okay? Had anyone else survived the attack?

Movement above brought her out of her thoughts and back to what was happening. She had no idea how long she had been unconscious, but it was still dark and the air had grown chilly. Were the same people who attacked the compound still there? Was she hearing surviving members of her clan returning to search for anyone else who might have survived? She wanted to peek out, to find out who was moving about, but her fear kept her pressed tight on the ledge.

"I need some help. There's someone under this rubble." Along with the scrapes and thuds of boards being shifted came a shower of dust.

"Don't…it's going to collapse." She coughed as the thick air got into her lungs.

"She's alive." A man knelt by the opening above her head. "Miss, are you injured?"

"Nothing broken." She glanced up but couldn't make out who was above her. "If you're going to kill me, just do it."

"What's your name?"

"I…" She stammered, unsure if she wanted to answer him. "Ivy."

"I'm Ty, the Alpha of the Alaskan Tigers. We're here to help. Give us a moment and we'll have you out of there."

The Queen of the Tigers' mate was there for her. He'd come to save them, or at least find out if anyone survived. Mason had been right. Committing to Tabitha in her new role as Queen would save their people. What Ivy didn't understand was why the rogues were so against it. If the prophecy was right, and Tabitha was killed before she could continue her family's line, all of the tiger shifters would die with her. Why would the rogues bring about their own death? She understood some were certifiably insane, but from the research she had done on Randolph, she didn't believe he was. So what was his reason behind all of this? What was he getting out of it?

A bit of falling debris made her cough. The people above her seemed closer. While she'd been weighing what was going through Randolph's mind, Ty and the others had apparently been working to clear a passage to her. Through their muffled voices she caught enough to let her know they were discussing the best way to get her out without the rest of the house collapsing on top of her.

"Ivy, would you be able to stand?" Another deeper voice called to her; this time it wasn't Ty.

"I think, but I couldn't reach enough to climb out. It's too far."

"If you can stand, I should be able to grab you and pull you up."

She tried to wiggle enough to get her feet under her so she could stand, but instantly pain shot through her hand. "I think my wrist is broken. I won't be much help."

"Just hang tight. We'll put plan B into operation."

"Plan B?"

"I'm coming down to get you."

"Oh no…I'm just balanced on a piece of floor that didn't go with the rest of the house. It's not strong enough for two. We'll fall."

"Don't worry, I'm not going to get on the ledge and we're not going to let you fall. Just give me a few minutes and I'll have you out of there," he called down, and then he mumbled something she couldn't make out to someone up top.

"Don't risk yourself."

"We're not going to let you stay down there," Ty hollered. "Carran's about to come down to you. Do exactly what he tells you, and we'll have you up here in just a moment."

"Ty…are there any other survivors?"

"We haven't found any." At his words, a soft moan escaped her lips, and as if he heard it, he added, "But that doesn't mean they didn't get away. Maybe some are in hiding, and we just haven't found them yet."

"Do you think the rogues were successful in their plan to eliminate Mason and his guards?" She tried to keep her voice even, but it was impossible; she heaved, trembling as she bit her bottom lip to keep from sobbing.

"I don't know, but we've got people looking." Ty paused for a moment. "Your brother is the Captain of Guards for Mason, isn't he?"

"Yes." She wanted to rant about the position and the danger of it, but Ty wasn't the person to bitch to. Not when he routinely risked his own life to save others.

"We haven't found any trace he was one of the members killed tonight. It's possible he escaped maybe even with Mason. I know it's not much, but it's all I have at the moment. Keep faith and if he's out there my team will find him."

"Thank you." Her voice was soft as she blinked away the tears.

Not being able to reach her pocket, she slipped her cell phone into her bra and brought her legs up to her chest. She wanted to be ready for whatever she had to do. It wouldn't be safe to linger and risk the ledge breaking.

Minutes later, a man's feet appeared, the scuffs and scars on his heavy boots visible in the dim light that followed his progress. He drew near and a board fell from above, barely missing her rescuer, then clattered to the rubble below.

"Cover your head the best you can."

She placed her good hand over her head, leaving enough room that she could look up at him. Even through the darkness she could make out his midnight black hair streaked with charcoal—not the gray of age but more like highlights.

"Ivy, I'm Carran, I'm part of the guard team for the Alaskan Tigers' Elders."

"Maybe you'd like to dispense with the introductions until she's on solid ground," Ty hollered. "The guys up here can't hold this structure forever, so unless you want it to fall on your heads, hurry up."

"What I need you to do is just stand up, nice and slow," Carran directed. "I don't want you to use your wrist at all, just let me worry about holding on to you once I grab you."

Carefully, she forced her legs under her, the beam crumbling away as she did. The pain from her stomach forced her to touch it, to see if she could feel any glass. She pulled her hand away and from the light on Carran's harness she could see blood coating her fingers and covering the front of her shirt. Slowly she eased the material up, her fingers shaking. "Oh, shit…"

"You're fine. Look at me."

"Fine? I've been shot!" At the sight of the hole in her stomach, she wanted to vomit.

"Ivy, look at me," Carran demanded.

She forced her attention away from the wound. Weak, she leaned back against the wall and the ledge disintegrated beneath her feet just as he swooped in and grabbed her. Clinging to him she chanced a glance below, instantly regretting it. The jagged edges of the rubble meant she would die if he lost his hold on her.

"I don't want to die…not like this."

"You won't, I've got you. Wrap your legs around my waist and keep your head tucked against my body." Echoing bangs made her ears ring but she did as he asked. "Bring us up."

Unable to believe she had survived, she clung to him. She only hoped Chad had been just as lucky. *Chad, you'd better not have died on me…*

Bearing Secrets: Alaskan Tigers

Chapter Two

The Browns' Island was unlike any place in the world, offering the best of everything from pristine waters to mountain views. Turi Brown was one of the last brothers left in residence on the island; this was the home he never wanted to leave. If he could choose to be anywhere in the world forever, it would be the island.

In need of a break from family drama, he traipsed through the snow down to the dock. The sun was sinking low into the horizon, sending pinks and reds through the sky, casting a beautiful glow on the ocean. His mother once told him Alaska was the most beautiful place. Until he started traveling, completing missions both for his sleuth—bear clan—and the Alaskan Tigers, he never realized just how amazing the place was.

He slipped down onto one of the wood benches Theodore had crafted. In under two hours, the whole family would be gathered together again on the island. The eldest twins, Taber and Thorben, had already returned with their mate Kallie. Thaddeus, Milo, and their mate Courtney were on their way, along with the youngest of the Brown brothers, Theodore. Everyone in one place again.

It was going to be hell.

The brothers got along for the most part, but whenever they were together it always became a competition. It didn't matter what it was, they always tried to better the others. Who could run fastest, shift the quickest? Who was the best shot? They tried to outdo each other in every aspect of their lives. It was what boys did, but having a bear within each of them only made it worse.

Hearing footsteps crunching snow, he turned to find his twin standing just beyond the dock, in his typical attire of jeans and white T-shirt, with a black leather jacket. Trey and Turi were identical in every way, except when it came to the leather jacket. That was Trey's way of rebelling from their mother's control, using the jacket as his way of getting under her skin. Even as an adult he found pleasure in doing little things to annoy their parents, while Turi was the peacemaker, always trying to smooth things over.

"Mom's looking for you." Trey shoved his hands into the pockets of the leather jacket and stepped onto the dock.

Turi looked back out at the water, trying to relax the anxiety that was charging the beast within. "I needed a bit of fresh air, she's driving me crazy."

"She wants everything to be perfect. It's the first time we'll all be home since before Taber and Thorben claimed their mate. This is the first time she'll meet her new daughter-in-law, Courtney. It's understandable she's on edge."

"You haven't had to deal with her since the crack of dawn. She was over at my place banging on the window to get me up so I could help her," Turi bitched.

"Why'd she let me sleep?"

"Dad and you didn't get back until late from inland. She wanted to make sure you were well rested, so you wouldn't be grumpy. That left me to be her service boy." He'd never known a homecoming could be so exhausting. "If she needs anything else done, you're her man, Trey."

"Nah, I think I'll stay down here with you for a bit." Trey strolled over, heaving a sigh as he took a seat next to him on the bench.

Turi glanced toward Trey and noticed the deep lines across his forehead. Something was up with his easygoing brother. "What's on your mind?"

"We're next…"

"Don't go there." He shook his head not willing to think about it.

"Seriously, Turi. Dad said he and his brothers found their mates in the order they were born. If the pattern holds, we're next."

"I heard you the first time, you don't need to repeat it," he snapped. "Maybe it won't be for a while."

"You mean because Travis would have been next if Taber hadn't killed him to protect Kallie." Trey leaned forward, placing his elbows on his knees, and met Turi's gaze.

Turi didn't want to think about how their own brother had turned against them and went after Kallie for a payout. "It's possible."

"We need to think about what is more likely…" He paused before glancing back at Turi. "I know you don't want to hear it, but it's likely we'll end up with the same mate. Just as Taber and Thorben did."

"You're right. I don't want to think about that." Turi pushed off the bench and strolled farther down the dock. "It might work for them but for us…"

"It won't work," Trey agreed.

"No." He ran his hand through his hair, sending the brown strands the wind had blown away from his face. "Let's face it, Trey. We were never even able to share a toy growing up. How are we supposed to share a woman? We fight over the stupidest shit sometimes."

"I see you're going to make this all my fault. It's impossible to share with you, you're possessive. That's why we couldn't share a mate."

"Me, possessive? Are you insane? That's you." Turi laughed at the irrational idea. "What about the fact you've never been able to finish a single thing you've started? You want to cruise through life like it owes you something. You're not a teenager, yet you still do the things you know are bound to get under our parents' skin."

"What about you? That shifter forum we were going to do, you didn't stick with that. Nothing's ever as important to you as rushing off the island to save the day with Dad or the Alaskan Tigers."

"You could have done it, I wasn't stopping you. It was a good idea but when do *I* have the time?" Turi turned to face him. "There used to be time for everything I enjoyed. Instead, I'm stuck helping Dad and the others while you keep to yourself. This world doesn't own you anything, Trey. If I'm supposed to share a mate with anyone I need it to be someone I can trust to keep her safe, someone I *know* will have my back through all the shit that's coming. With this attitude of yours, it couldn't be you."

"The forum was ours, it seemed wrong to do it without out you." The disappointment sank Trey's shoulders. "What do you plan to do about the mating, then? It's not like it's something we can change."

"Do my best *not* to find the one we're destined to be with." He had no other ideas how to avoid it, except to stay away from anyone who could possibly be meant for them. What Tad had said when they were protecting Courtney came back to him. *Once you've found your destined mate, nothing can stop you from claiming her, not even the idea of sharing her with Trey.*

"Logically, she'll fall into our laps. We should be ready."

"Ready?" Turi slid his hands into the pockets of his jeans to hide the anger that had balled them into fists. "Then maybe you should realize it's time to do more for the sleuth than the bare minimum."

"I've been there whenever anyone needs me," Trey defended.

"Yeah, when someone *calls* you. If you inserted yourself more to the sleuth and shifter business…" Turi kick a stick off the dock, sending it into the water. "Forget it."

"No, say it. I'm a failure."

"You're not a failure…" Turi shook his head. He never thought of his brother as a failure, just a slacker.

"But?" Trey prodded.

"You could do more. With Tabitha claiming her place as the Queen of the Tigers and the uneasiness that's rippling through the shifter population, it's a dangerous time for all of us, not just the tiger shifters."

"How did we get so wrapped up in the Alaskan Tigers' drama?"

"They came to help us when we needed it. Now we're there for them. Plus with Taber, Thorben, and Tad all mated with tigers, how could we turn our backs on them even without our past?"

"Family." Trey nodded. "You're right, I could do more."

"Then do it. With the others at the Alaskan Tigers' compound, Dad and I could use all the help we can get."

"What can I do?"

"Let's see if you're up for the challenge." Turi joked. "Tad still blames himself for what happened to Rosemarie, and he does his best to keep away from Aunt Bev, but with the family gathering tonight it's going to be hard. Can you help make sure things don't get out of hand with them?"

"You think there's going to be problems?"

Turi shrugged. "It's possible, Aunt Bev has been through a lot. First Rosemarie killed by those trespassing hunters, and then she thought she lost John because he was with Travis the night he was killed."

"John's a follower. He always respected Travis and when John thought he needed help, he followed. John never suspected Travis to betray his sleuth, and go after his brothers' mate."

"It's lucky John wised up or he'd be dead, and our sleuth would have lost two." Turi's lips curled up into a smile. "You realize this is the first time we've actually talked without bickering in months?"

"Yeah, it might give Mom a heart attack," Trey teased as he lowered himself back onto the bench. "We've had a few rough spots in the past, but we've got to find solid ground to build on. I know you're against us sharing a mate, but if that's our destiny then there's nothing we can do about it. I want to find her. I'm tired of the single life."

"Let's take this one step at a time. You start doing more for the sleuth and we'll see about building what we once had." Turi tipped his head back and looked up at the sky. "Sharing a mate won't be easy."

"Nothing worth having is easy." Trey turned on his heel and headed back toward the cabins.

Turi stood there by the water, his thoughts in turmoil. There was more tension between him and his twin than there had been for years. It was sickening. They had never been as close as some twins, but they were brothers. Somehow he'd have to find the solid ground between them again. With a silent curse for being born a twin and destined to share a mate, he made his way back to the house. They had a family celebration to attend.

Chapter Three

As the helicopter came over the mountains and the Brown Island came into view, Ivy couldn't stop herself from hating how her life had turned out. As a lone human surrounded by shifters, she had a poor idea of what normal life was like. And there was danger everywhere she turned. Despite this, she couldn't separate herself from it. Not after the good she'd witnessed, the people she had met.

"You'll be safe here while we figure out what to do next." Ty glanced back at her from the co-pilot's chair. "The Brown family will protect you while we find your brother."

"I should be out there looking for him."

"You've been shot," Ty reminded her as if the searing pain wasn't a continual reminder. "You're not a shifter and you need time to heal. This is no time for you to go traipsing through who-knows-what to find Chad. Let us worry about that."

"I know, but sitting around doing nothing isn't my style."

"One of the brothers will have a laptop you can use and you can get back to your…stuff."

Stuff. She shook her head. "I was putting together a proposal of why there needs to be a group of shifters banding together to keep law and order. So that what happened in Ohio and Texas doesn't repeat itself."

"That's why Tabitha is taking her position as Queen of the Tigers."

She adjusted the microphone on the headset so she could be sure Ty heard her over the whipping of the helicopter. "I'm not just concerned with the tigers but with all shifters. It has to be happening across the board, in other breeds. I'm aware not all shifters live in groups like the tigers do, but there're still problems for everyone. No group is spared from the rogue issues."

Ty nodded. "You're right, but now I think we have all the problems we can manage. Give us time and we'll move to a shifter-wide solution. We have to be able to show the other breeds we've made this work. It won't happen overnight, but there's a future with the shifters and humans living side by side. That's what we're all working toward."

"It's what I thought my clan wanted too," she whispered, more to herself than anyone else as Adam brought the helicopter down.

"The Alpha of the Arizona Tigers did want that."

"Do you think he's dead?" She knew the Alpha well, but that wasn't her reason for asking. If Mason was dead, it was likely her brother was as well, since he was the Captain of Mason's guards. *Damn him! I warned him against taking the position as an Elder guard. He couldn't just be happy and live a quiet life. He always had to risk everything.*

Ty glanced back at her with sadness in his gaze. "It's likely. The rogues would have gone after Mason first. Their first objection would have been to eliminate him. That doesn't mean Chad is gone though."

It was nice he tried to put her mind at ease, but she knew the risks of his job. It would have been Chad's responsibility to defend Mason to the death. The only way he'd have been able to get out of it, without being a traitor, was if there'd been a direct challenge to the Alpha to take over the clan. Even then, it couldn't have been a challenge by a true rogue; it would have to be a lone shifter or one devoted to a clan. There was only a slim possibility Chad hadn't been there when it happened. He could have been attending to something else when shit hit the fan. If he was alive, where was he? He'd have come after her; there wasn't a chance he'd have left her to die if he could help it.

She pushed the thoughts and tears away and stepped out of the helicopter. There would be plenty of other time to regret not seeing what was coming. Now that she thought about it, there had been little hints online that something bad could be coming to those clans who agreed to follow Tabitha in her one-ruler plan. Back then, Ivy hadn't put the pieces together, and now it was too late. She couldn't save anyone.

"The Browns are celebrating…being together and the matings that have happened. In the world we live in, we must celebrate the little things," Ty explained as she hesitated at the sound of loud music.

"Then we shouldn't be here…we shouldn't intrude on this." She took a step backward, her hand reaching out behind her for the helicopter.

"This is the one place I know you'll be safe. They'll understand." Ty took a few more steps and when he realized she wasn't behind him, he paused. "Come along. This night isn't getting younger, and there are things I need to attend to after this."

"I just imagine there are. Your job is never done." She had learned long ago that the long hours Chad put in was only the surface of what an Alpha did.

"What are you doing crashing our party?" A man in jeans and a sapphire blue dress shirt strolled toward them. As he came down the slight incline, the last remaining light sparkled over the sun kissed highlights of his light brown hair. He stood almost seven feet tall, every part of his body was toned and tight. *Wow!*

"Turi." Ty held out a hand to the other man. "I need to speak with Devon."

Turi took hold of Ty's hand and nodded to Adam who had come around the helicopter to join them. "Dad's at the party, is there something I can help you with?"

Ty tipped his head in her direction. "This is Ivy. She needs somewhere safe to stay."

"Welcome, Ivy, to the Brown Island. I'm Turi. My father, Devon, is the Alpha of the Kodiak Bears." He smiled at her before turning his attention back to Ty. "You know the sleuth is always willing to help, but we need to know the story. We can't get into this without knowing what it's about."

"Ivy was a member of the Arizona Tigers. There was an attack on her compound, dispensing the clan, and we fear she could be in danger. Those who weren't killed turned rogue and joined Randolph's ranks. We're concerned because of her position within the clan and the project she was working on, that if Randolph finds out she's alive he'll seek to eliminate her. Having her here is the safest place while we find her brother," Ty explained.

Turi glanced between her and Ty. "She's human."

"I'm right here. Could you please not speak like I'm an idiot who can't understand you?" She couldn't keep the anger out of her voice. Taking a deep breath, she quickly ran down the answers of the questions she knew he would ask. "Yes, I'm human. It's a long story. No, I wasn't mated to anyone in the clan. My brother is a shifter and was the Captain of the Guards for the Alpha."

Turi's eyes widened for a moment before he finally nodded. "My apologies. There's a party going on, why don't you join us? I'll introduce you to the family."

"If you agree Ivy can stay here, then Adam and I need to return. I have a team following leads for Chad and the other Elders now, but we should get back."

"You think—" Turi stopped mid-sentence and glanced toward her.

"Chad could be dead," she finished tersely.

"We don't know, and until we do we'll search for him or a clue he's dead. He could have been hurt and found a safe place to wait and heal," Ty explained before he leaned toward Turi and kept his voice low. "It's unlikely, so try to keep her realistic."

"This is becoming ridiculous." She stepped away from the helicopter and toward Ty. "I don't have the spidery senses you guys do, so I have to rely on what I do. Since I have the hearing of a human, my lip reading skills are amazing."

The men turned to look at her, as if wondering where she was going with it. "I can read your lips. I know it's unlikely he's alive, but I know if anyone could survive it's Chad. So please stop treating me like a child, don't sugarcoat things, or leave me out of it because you think I can't handle it."

"I forgot to mention…Ivy is a live wire." Ty smirked. "She's feisty and hates when you keep things from her."

"My family and I will keep her safe. Do you need help?"

Ty shook his head. "Your mom has been waiting to have everyone here for some time, so we're not going to break up the party. Tomorrow, if we need it, but not today."

Adam sat the suitcase on the ground next to Ivy. "It's why we're not coming to the party. Your brothers will know something is wrong if we show up."

"Then you should go." Turi glanced back the way he came, as if looking for someone. "We heard the helicopter, so it won't be long before they come to see why I haven't come back."

"Adam, get the helicopter started," Ty ordered.

"You'll call if you have *any* news." Ivy dragged her hand through her hair until she was able to get all the loose strands away from her face.

"I'll call when I have something to report." Ty closed the distance between them and took her hand in his. "Don't go nagging the Browns for an update. You'll know when I have news."

"I won't make any promises." She glanced to the stud of a man, Turi. She had a feeling she was going to have more excitement here than in Arizona. "If I can get back to the project I was working on, it would give me something to keep me occupied, and maybe keep my mind off Chad."

"Turi, can you get Ivy a laptop to use while she's here?" Ty asked over the whipping of the helicopter blades. "Hers was blown up."

"Sure, first thing tomorrow." Turi reached down and grabbed the small suitcase Adam had set down. "If you'll come with me, I'll introduce you to the family."

"I'll be in touch." Ty told her just before he slipped into the helicopter next to Adam.

She moved back from the helicopter, feeling as if she'd just been cut off from the rest of the world. Surrounded by strangers on an island was not her idea of a good time. She had always been so shy, and new people made her nervous. "Maybe if you'll just show me to where I'll be staying, you can get back to your party."

"Wouldn't you like to come meet everyone? No one bites, I promise."

She shook her head, sending her blonde hair into her face again. "It's a family event, I don't want to intrude."

"You're not. Plus I'm sure you're hungry."

His mention of food won her over. "Okay, if you're sure it's all right," she relented, following him. After all, she was a guest. She had to be friendly.

"We won't stay long and then I'll get you settled so you can rest and heal."

"How…" She stopped in her tracks. "How did you know?"

"I can smell the gun powder, the blood, and faint traces of the healing magic. With the way you are carrying yourself, gingerly, it was an easy deduction. Your wrist was broken too. One of the healers must have started the healing process, but you still need to take it easy while your body does the rest."

"That's amazing."

He shrugged and started walking again. "It's a bear thing. For some reason bears can sense the healing magic when no other breeds can."

"Bears?" She called out to him, just as the party came into view. Before he could answer, she saw one. A giant brown bear…dancing. She blinked. "This can't be happening."

"That would be my twin, Trey."

"Bears? This can't be happening."

"What's wrong with bears?" He laid her suitcase on the porch of the nearby house before coming to stand next to her.

"I should be with a tiger clan." She let out a light chuckle as the bear started to sway his hips like he was a belly dancer. All she could think about was those stupid bears that danced to a song that stores sold around Valentine's Day. "Sorry, that was rude. I only meant Chad wouldn't look for me here."

"That's the point. No one will be able to find you."

"Chad is my brother." She wanted to glance at him, but she couldn't tear her gaze away from the dancing bear, still making his way through the dance area.

"Brother or not, his position put you in danger. Right now you need to be here so you're safe and can heal."

Her statement had come out wrong, making her feel slightly guilty. She had nothing against other shifters, she was just worried Chad wouldn't be able to find her if he was still alive. Would he think to contract the Alaskan Tigers? Maybe if Mason was alive, but otherwise she didn't think he'd have a reason to.

Chad, please find me...

Bearing Secrets: Alaskan Tigers

Chapter Four

Trey shook his big bear body for all it was worth, dancing over to his new sisters-in-law and giving them his version of a lap dance. He shook his fur in their face, slid his bear paws over their thighs, and roared. This was his way of welcoming them to the family, to let them know what they had really gotten themselves into.

Recently the Brown family had become all work and little play. So this party was more than just welcoming Kallie, Courtney, and Milo to the family. It was also a chance for all of them to have a good time, let their beasts out. He might have been the only one grooving around the makeshift dance floor in his bear form, but the night was young and the party was just getting started.

He swayed his hips to the motion, shaking his large body in front of her. The lap dance didn't have the same stunning sway of a naked body but this was more fun for him. Not to mention that if he was giving naked lap dances it would be a fight between his brothers and his mother as to who would have the privilege of killing him. His bet would be on his brothers since they were closer.

"Get your hairy ass out of my mate's face." Taber growled, and swatted Trey away.

Instead of fighting it, he moved down the line to Tad's mates, Courtney and Milo. Oh, how he loved to screw with Tad about mating with a tiger shifter and a human. Three very different people and attitudes all had to merge together in a mating bond, yet somehow they were making it work.

He swung his hairy arm around Courtney's waist and pulled her up against his bear form. Squeezed tight against him, she squealed. "Tad…"

"The more you fight the stronger he will hold." Tad warned her.

Trey lifted her off her feet and spun her around. "How am I supposed to relax when I'm being swung around by a thousand pound bear?"

"Trey…" Tad's voice held a warning.

Just to irritate his brother, he brought Courtney's hand to his mouth and licked the top of it. Letting out a deep growl, he set her back down.

"Now we'll have to work all night getting your scent off our mate." Milo bitched and pulled Courtney into his lap, snuggling his head into her neck.

Like that's a hardship. He spun around and shook his rear at Milo in a *kiss-my-ass* way. Screwing with his brothers was a way of life, but it also eased some of the tension between Tad and Aunt Bev. Even after the years since Rosemarie's passing, Tad still blamed himself.

Aunt Bev swore she didn't blame Tad but there was a glimmer of sadness in her eyes throughout the party. The new additions to the family served to remind her just how much she had lost when her only daughter was killed.

"Trey, quit shaking your big ass before they tear you to pieces," Turi hollered as he came toward Trey with a woman at his side.

Tight jeans caressed the curves of her body like a glove, while a loose low-cut tank top gave a teasing peek to her ample cleavage. The breeze sent her long blonde hair fanning around her and gave him the urge to tangle his fingers in it, but it was her sea green eyes that kept his attention locked on her.

Distracted by the gorgeous woman, he was no longer paying attention to his siblings and their mates, when Milo reached out and clawed Trey's backside. An earthshaking growl poured from him as he pulled away.

What the hell? Turning around, he glared at Milo.

"It would seem as if we've gained from our mating." Tad sat with his mates and started to explain. "Milo now has the ability to draw his tiger claws while remaining in his human form."

Trey slipped behind the stage, quickly pulling the energy and shifting back into his human form before donning his clothes again. "You bastard." He called to Milo as he came back around buttoning his jeans, his T-shirt stuck in his back pocket.

"You got what was coming to you." Milo smirked.

"I guess what they say is true…a cat's bite is nothing compared to its claws." Trey rubbed his hand over the ass cheek that now sported long, burning claw marks.

"Quit your bitching Trey, I'd like you to meet our guest, Ivy. She was a member of the Arizona Tigers and will be staying with us for the time being," Turi explained.

"Hello Ivy, welcome." Trey held out his hand to her. The instant their fingers met, the connection flared to life. Electricity poured through them, rushing in circles as it tried to find something. No…*someone*…Turi.

"Ivy?" Turi asked when she let out a soft moan.

Trey couldn't pull away or even speak before Turi laid his hand on Ivy's arm, closing the connection. Electricity stopped circling through them and poured into Turi. The connection complete, bringing all the emotions and thoughts from Ivy and Turi into him, transformed the three of them into one.

"Shit!" Both of the twins shouted at the same time, pulling away as if they'd been burned.

Turi was going to kill him. They had talked about the possibility of them having to share a mate only that morning. There was no way they were ready for it yet. He hadn't had time to prove he wasn't a lazy bear, that they could make it work.

"What just happened?" Ivy glanced between them.

"Boys…" Their mother's voice cut into them staring at each other. "There's no reason to do this here, take Ivy up to your house.

Ivy, once my boys explain, if you have any questions come back down and find me."

"Let's get some privacy." Turi started toward his cabin.

"They're right, it shouldn't be done here." Trey placed his hand on the small of her back, but once the current began to flow through him, he pulled away to hover just next to her without actually touching. He didn't need the electricity charging his blood any more than it already was. One of them had to keep a cool head and he had a feeling it should be him.

* * *

The warmth of the cabin helped chase away the chill that had settled over Ivy from being outside with only a tank top on. She had been dressed for the Arizona temperatures, not Alaska, and she was pretty sure there wasn't a long-sleeved shirt in her wardrobe, let alone her suitcase.

"Here." Trey grabbed a blanket off the back of the leather chair and wrapped it around her arms.

"Thank you." She grabbed the edges to keep it firmly around her. "Now, will one of you please tell me what the hell just happened?"

"Mating…" Turi sank into the chair farthest from where they were.

"No." She shook her head. "Mating is between *two* people. That was something else."

"Twins run in the family." Trey leaned against the back of the sofa nearest her. "Our Grandmother Annabell—our mother's mother—mated with twins, giving our mom two fathers. They sought high and low for a way to break their matting, anything to remove the connection between the three of them, to give each of them a chance to find their own woman."

"That's not how mating works." She shook her head, not wanting to believe what he was saying.

"For most couples you'd be right, there's only one destined mate for them. But there's something more to the twin connection."

"You mean like DNA?" she questioned.

"Partially." Trey nodded and glanced to Turi who was sitting there with his arms crossed over his chest. "Identical twins have the same DNA, which is why they can end up with the same mate."

"Our oldest brothers, Taber and Thorben, are twins and are mated to Kallie," Turi finally said.

"I thought it was rare for shifters to have twins." Her legs turned to wet noodles and she needed to sit. The two steps around Trey and to a chair felt like she was climbing a mountain. All of the night's activities were catching up to her.

"For most breeds, multiple babies are uncommon," Trey agreed.

"Were they able to find something to stop this?" Even as she asked the question, she figured out the answer. If there was a remedy for it, the other twins wouldn't be mated to one woman.

"There was nothing to find. The mating is what it is." Trey glanced at Turi and then back to her. "If the mating is denied, the longing for each other's touch becomes excruciating. Given long enough, the need will drive you insane, our beasts will begin to gain more and more control until we are unable to do anything but give in."

"What happened with your grandparents? I mean, I guess they gave in, but were they ever happy?" She needed to know what was in store for her.

"They were left with no choice other than to return," Turi answered, his voice cold, averting his gaze as if unable to look at her.

"But what kind of life did they have? If they searched for a cure, they must not have wanted to be with your grandmother."

"As Mom explained it, they both cared for her very much, but for them it was more of a challenge to win her. Which of them were better and could withstand the mating need the longest? It wasn't until our grandmother began to suffer from their actions that they wised up." Trey stood from the sofa and strolled over to the window. "In the end things worked out well for them. Our grandparents lived a very happy life together."

"Mom never told us any of this until Taber and Thorben mated with Kallie. She said there was no reason to because she wasn't sure it would happen to us. Our grandparents were gone before we were old enough to remember having two grandfathers." Turi crossed his arms over his broad chest.

She tugged the blanket around her shoulders tighter and tried to put her finger on what she was missing. While Trey seemed open to it, almost excited, Turi was the opposite. Since their brief touch, he had closed himself off. Even as he sat there, he had distanced himself from them. He couldn't look at either of them without what appeared to be anger in his eyes. What was she missing? Was there tension between the brothers, and how was that going to affect the mating?

Chapter Five

In the last twenty-four hours, Ivy's home had been blown up, her whole clan killed, and her brother was missing, along with the clan Elders. Now she'd been thrown onto an island with bears, and into a mating with twins who couldn't even look at each other. She wasn't up to a long discussion about whatever had caused the tension between them. Suddenly she realized all the tension between them would affect their mating. This sent her heart racing as the first waves out doubt lanced through her. The urge to run coursed through her body, uncertainty overtaking her. She hadn't known either of them very long, they had major issues to resolve between them; if this wasn't a red flag, she didn't know what was. Could she risk involving herself with these men?

Mating was something special, something she'd hoped would happen to her, because if she chose a life with a human she'd have to leave the clan. The clan wouldn't risk their secret to bring in another human they had no ties to. There would be no way to know where their loyalty lay, possibly until it was too late. A shifter mate would allow her to stay within the shifter folds, and close to her brother, friends, and the people she considered family.

Bears? I always thought it would be a tiger. Bears weren't really what she had in mind, but destiny hadn't given her a choice. This was hers to claim and she needed to claim it with both hands. With or without the red flag. In order to accept what she desired, she needed to figure out what the underlying tension was from.

"What am I missing? Turi, why can't you look at either of us?"

"Don't get upset. It's nothing against you." Trey stood up for his brother when Turi didn't answer. "Over the years I've done things within the family that have caused problems. Turi was the one who suffered the most for them."

"Damn right, Trey." Turi shot out of the chair, the anger pouring off him. "I spent my life covering for you, picking up on your slack. You're my brother so I've done it, plus it was for the best of the sleuth, but I won't do it when it comes to mating. I'm not going to have to share a mate with you when I know you'll end up hurting her, and I'll be left trying to keep her from hating us both."

"I told you—"

Turi waved a hand, cutting him off. At the same time he took a step forward, rage etching a scowl on his face. "Don't! I've heard it all before."

She pushed off the sofa, putting herself between them. "Hold on. I don't know what the hell happened between you two and honestly I don't care. That's for you to work out, but you're not going to come to blows here. Let's sit down and talk about this rationally."

Turi stepped back, the anger still clinging to him, but he relaxed his fists. "I need some air."

"Then get some, and when you're ready we'll be in here." With a mixture of irritation and understanding, she watched him walk away. She couldn't help but wonder if that would be a staple point of this mating.

The door clicked shut while Trey leaned against the wall, his gaze on the floor, unable to look at her. "I'm sorry."

"Every family has problems." Her statement made it sound so simple, yet it was anything but.

"This isn't fair to you to be drawn into this."

Shivering, she took a step back and sat down on the sofa. "Why don't you tell me what the problem is between you two?"

With one last glance out the window, he moved away from it, and to the fireplace. Crouching next to a pile of wood, he grabbed a couple of small logs and tossed them into the dying embers. Keeping his back to her, he grabbed the poker and stirred the fire until the new logs caught. "I've always been the troublemaker of the family. Take my leather jacket for instance." He nodded toward the chair where he'd casually tossed it. "I started wearing it because it drove Mom nuts. I just gave a lap dance in my bear form to Kallie, Courtney, and Milo to welcome them to the family. What kind of welcome is that?"

"A big Kodiak bear giving a lap dance, shaking your furry body…come on, Trey, that was adorable." She smirked, remembering the way his bear form moved. *Maybe he'll give me a lap dance in all his manly glory.*

"Turi didn't find it too amusing." He shoved the poker back into the holster. "He just saw it as another way I wasn't falling into line. It didn't matter that I dispelled the tension with Tad and Aunt Bev earlier. All he could see was I wasn't him."

"Fall into line?" She decided to stick with one problem and leave the comment about Tad and Bev for later.

"Taber and Thorben are the oldest, they are supposed to take over the sleuth when the time comes for Dad to step down, but they live full time at the Alaskan Tigers' compound. They're there to help the Elders Ty and Raja and because their mate feels safe there. Tad is mated to Courtney—a human—and Milo one of the guards for the Alaskan Tigers' Lieutenant's mate Bethany, so they've taken up residence at the compound too. It leaves Turi and me as the next oldest, to assist Dad with the sleuth responsibilities."

She raised an eyebrow, unable to believe what she was hearing. "Are you telling me Turi thinks you can't do your duties because you like to push the limits, play some jokes, and have a good time?"

"Turi is very much by the book, even if that book is an unwritten one. He's all business. To him I'm slacking off, and sliding through life like it owes me something." He sank down by the fireplace and sat on the hearth. "To him there's no balance, it's all work and no play. I guess that's why I've always been the one to push things further. I needed to make up for the stick in his ass."

"I have a brother just like that." She laughed and the tension from the day slipped away. "Chad's the Captain of Guards for my Alpha…well, former…"

"Don't." He reached out to her, placing his hand over hers. The touch brought the connection back to life. "We don't know anything has happened to them. They could have escaped and might be in hiding."

"Isn't this cozy." She turned to find Turi standing just behind them, the disgust dripping from each word. "I step outside for a few minutes and you start laying your claim."

"Turi…" The rage in his eyes made her want to go to him, to lay her hand on his arm and calm the storm raging within him. The anger called his beast to the surface, making the situation dangerous. One wrong move and his bear would come out howling. That very thought kept her at bay more than the way his body screamed for her to stay away.

Bearing Secrets: Alaskan Tigers

Chapter Six

Entering the cabin to find Trey and Ivy in a cozy exchange exploded the rage within Turi. He had no right to be jealous, since he was the one who'd stepped out, but it didn't change what was pouring through him like burning lava. Jealousy of his own brother seemed irrational, when they were supposed to share her, but that changed nothing. Hadn't he just vowed he'd run as far and as fast from a mating where he was expected to share? Now here he was being drawn to her.

Trey narrowed his eyes. "You're the one who left instead of facing what destiny has dropped on our doorstep."

"Hold on." She laid her free hand over Trey's, running her fingers along his knuckles. "Trey, could you give me a few minutes? I heard your side, now I need to hear his."

Trey glanced between Turi and Ivy before finally nodding. "I'll be outside, holler when you want me." He rose from the fire and went outside without another word.

She adjusted on the sofa, turning toward him. "Trey explained you think he's too relaxed, but even with that I don't understand this anger you seem to have."

Turi growled. "For years I've picked up the slack when it came to the sleuth, but I'm not going to do it when it comes to mating. I don't want my mate to look at me and see hatred for what my brother has done. Before you deny it, we're identical. It would be impossible for you not to look at me and be reminded of the ways he let you down."

"Identical in looks, maybe, but your personalities are so different."

"Looks are enough to remind you." He had spent years proving himself to the sleuth, even to his own family.

She shook her head. "But I don't see it that way."

"In time you will." He stood his ground, because he knew just what Trey was capable of.

"Fine." She tossed the blanket off her shoulders and stood. "What are you going to do about it then? Obviously you don't want this mating, so why don't you find a cure for this? Surely things have changed since the days of your grandparents."

Damn, she was feisty. He placed his elbows on the back of the leather chair and leaned forward, watching her. Was she trying to call his bluff? Did she truly want him to find something that would fix their situation? It would give her a chance to live a normal life, with one person—maybe a human.

"Maybe there is." He nodded. If she was about to call him on not wanting to share her with Trey, she had another thing coming. "Taber and Thorben just took Mom's word for it. Is that what you want? Do you want me to find something so you can live a normal life…with a human?"

"Obviously, what I want doesn't play into this. You already have your mind made up. So why are you still here?"

He stepped around the chair and stalked toward her. "I'm here because of you. Damn it, you have to feel it. This draw to you is overpowering, just being out on the porch was too far from you. You're human but you should feel the connection."

"Oh, I feel it for both of you." She cupped his cheek. "Which leaves us with two options. Either you two have to find a cure before this need burns me alive from the inside, or work out your problems. I won't be a ping-pong ball between you two. A mating is hard enough, let alone having two mates who can barely stand each other."

Unable to stop his bear from wanting to feel her, he slipped his arm around her waist. "To think only this morning Trey and I had the conversation about mating. He knew we'd be next and wanted to fix the problems between us. Neither of us figured you'd drop into our laps tonight."

"Next?"

"Dad and his brothers were all mated in order of their birth, and so far it's been like that for us. First the first set of twins Taber and Thorben, then Tad, and now us. Poor Theodore is the last one."

The back door opened, sending a cold gust of wind through the cabin. "Where's Trey?"

"Mom—"

"Don't 'Mom' me, boy." His mother glared at him. "I came to see how things were going. Where's your brother?"

"He's on the porch, I'll get him." He pulled his arm from around Ivy's waist. "Ivy, this is our mother, Ava, don't let her growl scare you. She only ever sinks those claws into Dad."

"You're not too old for me to claw you up," she hollered as he went to get Trey.

He pulled open the door, quickly spotting Trey pacing the porch like a caged animal. "Come back inside, Mom's here," he told him before strolling back to where the women waited.

"Did my boys explain what happened down at the party?" Ava sank down onto one of the leather chairs.

"Yes ma'am." Ivy nodded.

"No 'ma'am' here. Either Mom or Ava, you're family now." She glared at the boys. "Unless these idiot sons of mine are planning to do something stupid."

"I don't know…"

"No Mom, nothing stupid." Turi glanced at Trey. "I don't know how we're going to do this, but somehow we'll have to make it work."

"I'm glad I don't have to remind you of the consequences for not claiming your mate. The pain wouldn't just happen to the two of you, but also to Ivy. She's human, so it would be harder for her to handle. She would feel like it's burning her alive and in the end it would essentially do that. It's not something I want to see any of you endure."

"Yes Mom, we know the consequences," Turi and Trey said together.

Ava glanced at Ivy. "Then I guess all that's left to discuss is how Ivy came to know about shifters. It's not common for a human to know about us, and less common for one to have a shifter sibling."

"Mom, I don't think this is the time." Turi shook his head. "She's been through a lot today. Let her get some rest, and we can discuss that tomorrow."

"Very well, I should get back to the party anyway." Ava stood, ran her hand down the front of her dress, shaking away invisible wrinkles, and looked at Ivy. "We're having a family brunch tomorrow with his brothers and their mates. I'd appreciate it if you could be there. It's rare the whole family is together, and most of them will be leaving soon. I'd like to have us all together while I can."

Ivy nodded. "We'll be there."

Ava smiled. "Thank you. See you in the morning." She left, leaving them with the question of Ivy's past still hanging in the air.

"You're right, I am tired but first I think you need to know." She dragged her hand through her hair before leaning back against the sofa.

"Only if you want," Trey told her as he sat next to her.

Turi smirked. "For once I agree with him. Our past is just that. In the past. It brought us here, but it doesn't play into the future."

"Actually, I think it might."

Turi looked to Trey, confusion knitting his brow, before nodding to Ivy. "Go ahead." He wanted to hear whatever she thought was important, but he knew it wouldn't change the mating that had already started between them.

Chapter Seven

Unable to sit still, Ivy paced the cozy living area, staying near the fire and its warmth while keeping a little distance between her and the brothers. She was about to bare a secret of her past that only two people in her life knew—Chad and Mason. There was a reason it had been kept a secret for all these years. Now she had to tell her mates and possibly their family. What if it got out? Even if it were leaked to just one person…he'd find her.

With no other choice, she took a deep breath and swallowed her fears. Her mates had a right to know what they were getting themselves into, even if they didn't have a choice to run.

"Ivy, whatever it is, you can tell us." Trey reached out to her but she slipped away just before he could lay his hand on her.

"I'm sorry…" Even without the mating finalized, the pain of turning from him gnawed at her stomach. "If you touch me now, I'll never get it out."

"Tell us, so we can help you," Turi urged. He wrung his hands, clearly uneasy and wanting to help.

"There's no easy way to say this, so I'll just put it out there. On the way here Ty told me a little about your...well, I thought *clan* at the time since he forgot to mention you're bears." She ran her hands through her hair, pulling the blonde strands into a messy ponytail and used one of the elastic holders from her wrist. "He told me your sleuth has been assisting with the rogue tiger issues, first with Pierce, and now with Randolph."

Turi straightened in his seat; she clearly had his attention. "Yes. We were on the mission with Ty when Pierce was killed."

"Then you're aware Randolph has taken over where Pierce has left off?" The twins exchanged a glance and then nodded. "He's my uncle."

"He's *what?*" Turi nearly shouted, popping out of the chair like a demented jack-in-the-box.

Tears filled her eyes, threatening to spill over, and Turi's agitation wasn't helping. She moved away from the fireplace, going anywhere she could so she didn't have to look at the hurt in Turi's eyes. It was as if she had betrayed them because of her heritage. She had been brought into it, she didn't choose it.

"Hey." Trey stepped in front of her, cutting off her escape path, and reached his hand out to her, his fingers gliding along her arm, caressing her tentatively. "It's okay."

"Okay? How can it ever be okay?" She nodded back at Turi. "Look at how he took the news. If anyone finds out, they'll look at me the same way. Like I had something to do with Randolph's actions, or that I have the same views he did. I've been raised in the

Arizona clan my whole life, I'd never do what he's done, or even think about it."

"I didn't think you would." His voice was low and soothing. "Now come here and explain how he's your uncle." Trey slid his arm around her waist, pulling him against his body. "Turi's not going to say anything." He shot a glance at his brother, giving him a *shut-the-hell-up* look.

"Randolph and my mother were siblings. Their parents were a mixed couple, a tiger and a human. According to my mother, my grandmother always despised the fact she had to spend her life with a shifter, and passed her hatred on to her son...Randolph. It's strange because even though he was a shifter, she didn't show him half as much hatred as she showed her husband. Maybe she knew that she'd breed a monster with her hate, one who would fight against shifters as a whole. He was her only chance to bring down the group she despised so much." She kept her gaze on Trey, taking strength from him, while ignoring Turi. "My mother was the second born and human. Neither of her parents paid much attention to her. To her father, she was a lesser being, and her mother was so devoted to pass on her hatred to Randolph she didn't care about my mother."

"Go on, angel," Trey provoked when she paused.

"My mother had a rough pregnancy, and she wasn't expected to live through my birth. Chad's mother, Kathy, was her best friend...when my mother passed away, Kathy took me in and raised me as her own daughter. I knew my aunt as my mother and Chad as my brother until I was in my early teens. That's when she explained everything me. After she died, only Chad and Mason knew. We kept the secret in order to keep me hidden from Randolph. To keep my heritage hidden from everyone, even him. I don't believe he knows. When Kathy took me in and told Mason my heritage, they decided to make sure it remained a secret."

"Does he know you're alive?" Turi asked.

"I don't know…" She pressed her head against Trey's chest. "It's possible, I guess. All I know is that we kept it secret because if he knew I existed, he'd kill me."

"Damn right he would. He wants to see all tiger shifters dead," Turi growled.

"Because of the hatred my grandmother hand-fed him morning, noon, and night, like it was candy," she clarified, her voice breaking.

"My angel." Trey waited until she looked up at him. "Your heritage doesn't matter."

"Like hell it doesn't matter." Turi exploded, jumping to his feet and beginning to pace. "She's a direct link to Randolph. He'll come after her if he finds out who she is."

"My dear brother…" Trey looked over her head and watched Turi. "You always handle the curve balls that life throws at you, but you're not handling this one very well."

"It's one thing after another." Turi shook his head. "You're right. I'm not handling this well and it's not your fault, Ivy, it's mine. I'm sorry. I know the damage Randolph has done, and to think he could be after you—my mate—is terrifying. It's one thing to have to go up against him when it's to protect someone else but when it's about protecting my own, it's entirely different."

"What if he knew? Maybe that's the reason he attacked the clan…" Her legs gave out under her, if it wasn't for Trey's hand on her waist she'd have collapsed into a heap on the floor.

"What is it, angel?" Trey tightened his grip on her waist, keeping her standing.

"When I was hiding…someone was there. I overheard him on the phone with Randolph. *The clan's been eliminated. We'll be ready to move on the next clan in a few days.*" She repeated the words as they played through her mind again. "It was an assassination, not just for Mason but for my whole clan. They're dead…"

"You don't know that. Chad and the other guards could have gotten Mason to safety," Turi reasoned.

"No…" She buried her head in Trey's chest. "He'd have come back to find me."

"Only after he got Mason to safety." Turi's footsteps echoed on the hardwood floor, nearing her. "He'd have done his duty and got Mason somewhere safe. As the Captain of the Guards, he'd have to do what was needed, especially if the other Elder guards didn't survive."

"I want to believe you, but it's unlikely."

"It's hard to kill our kind, so until we know for certain, just try to think positive." Trey smoothed his hand over her back. "Ty's got a team out there looking for them, we should know something soon."

Not soon enough...

Chapter Eight

Music and laughter drifted through the air from the party that was still in full swing when Turi wandered out to the deck with a bottle of beer in hand. The wrap-around deck had been one of his favorite features of the home; it was one of the special touches none of the other cabins had. Since his place sat on a slight incline, the deck allowed him to take advantage of all the views.

The views...

He cursed and took a long swig from his beer. For the first time, he didn't see the magnificence of the area, the beautiful water or the snowcapped mountains. All he could see was how dangerous their world had become. His life was about the missions, taking down rogues, saving the innocent, eliminating abusive Alphas, helping to heal those who needed it. That wasn't the life he wanted a mate to be surrounded with, let alone children. Never knowing if he'd make it back alive—what kind of life was that for a family?

Ty and his clan had backed the Kodiak Bears when they needed it the most, and now, not only did the Brown brothers feel it was their duty to help him, but it was also something they wanted. The idea of living in a world where shifters were safe, no longer terrified of what might happen if their secret became known, was heavenly. It was the reason each of the brothers were ready at a moment's notice whenever Ty called. They were fighting for a better world for future generations.

At least that was what he had thought up until now. In that moment, he wondered if living in secret was such a bad thing. He had grown up happy and healthy on the island, never longing to mix with humans on the mainland. Being on the island had given him a childhood he knew many didn't have. He'd been safe and there were no hunters trying to eliminate them. Bear shifters were different from others; normally they were able to shift by their first birthday whereas tiger shifters had to pass through a transition phase normally in their early teens. At that age they didn't understand the risks, and they needed a safe place to be raised in case of an accidental shift.

While watching his family celebrate, he leaned forward on the wooden banister and wondered if all the fighting was worth it. Was all the blood, death, and risk really worth it in the end? What would happen when they came out to the world? Would there be more threats? Instead of just having to worry about Randolph and the rogues, would there be hunters trying to win a shifter skin for their trophy room?

Behind him, the screen door creaked and the thump of boots neared. Even knowing Trey was standing behind him, Turi couldn't pull his gaze away from the party. He didn't know what to say to his brother. The anger that flowed through him over finding their mate now wasn't Trey's fault, it was destiny.

"She's finally resting." Trey came to stand next to Turi, keeping his back to the party. "I'm sorry."

"This isn't your fault." Turi ran his hand through his hair. "This is supposed to be a time of celebration. If finding your mate is supposed to be joyful then why do I feel so anxious?"

"You've always been the worrier of the family." Trey took a swig of his beer before looking at Turi. "Mating will help eliminate some of the unease."

"It's not just about mating. Do you ever wonder if what we're doing is really worth it? Maybe we're doing more harm than good. All the blood and death…what kind of life is that for her?"

"It's the only life if we want to make this a better world for our children."

"Why? So hunters can start collecting our skin, instead of actual bears? Or maybe so our mates and children have to live in fear that we won't come back from the latest goddamn mission?" He slammed his beer bottle down onto the banister sending liquid sloshing around inside. "Look at them down there celebrating, but we're not celebrating mating…we're actually celebrating that we're still alive. That the only one who was killed by this stupid war was Travis and that was due to his own betrayal."

"What happened to you? You've always believed in the cause."

"Maybe I've seen too much blood and death to believe any longer." Turi had to loosen his grip on the banister, or leave grooves from his fingers in the handcrafted wood.

"I think it might have something to do with that beautiful blonde that just strolled into our lives."

Turi wanted to beat the smirk right off Trey's face, but he was partially right. "All this danger was fun when we had nothing to worry about, but now all of us except Theodore are mated. If something happened to us, we'd leave behind a widow."

"That's the risk we all take, including the tigers." Trey set his beer aside. "Think of the good we've done and the lives we've saved. That's what should keep us getting up each morning to fight another day."

"Don't forget the lives we've lost. The innocents we were too late to save."

"Turi, why are we having this conversation? You and I both know that little woman in the house is going to keep us fighting. If we don't then how will we keep her safe? We have to eliminate Randolph and deal with the other rogues."

"After Randolph there will be another one. It will never end. Our battle for freedom from the shadows has only just begun, and I'm already tired."

"Tired is one thing, but what you're not doing is giving up. She's depending on us and I don't care if you hate me, we're not letting her down."

The unusual authority in Trey's voice had Turi turning to him in surprise. "I don't hate you."

"You just wish I was more like you."

"Sometimes, but when you were with Ivy I realized there was so much more to you. You comforted her while I was being an ass." He dragged his hand through his hair. "Maybe we're two sides of the same coin. You show the fun and softer side that I keep hidden, while I'm the one always worried about the next threat and I'm always business."

"Have you considered that might be the reason you doubt all of this now?" When Turi didn't answer, Trey added, "Don't worry, Ivy and I will help you let your wild side loose."

"Dad won't know what to do if I start acting like you," Turi teased. "Speaking of Dad, we'll have to tell him, but no one else can know about Ivy's heritage. I'm sure the sleuth will handle it better than I did, but we need to keep it as quiet as we can. Anyone else who might know is a risk to us and in danger themselves."

"I think the immediate family has a right to know. Taber, Thorben, Tad, and Theodore are out there risking their lives every day to make this world better for all of us. We're key players when it comes to taking down Randolph. They need to know the whole story."

"We'd be putting them in more danger."

"They're already in danger. So they should know so they can act accordingly. Mom should know too."

Turi relented with a nod. "We'll tell them in the morning, let them enjoy the party tonight."

"Don't you think Ty must know?"

"I don't know, but we're going to find out just how much he does." Turi grabbed the beer bottle he'd set aside earlier and polished off the last gulp. "You did well tonight with Tad and Aunt Bev."

"Thanks." Trey gave Turi one of his trademark grins, sending a twinkle to his eyes. "They've got to work out their problems eventually."

"There's no problem except Tad's guilt. Aunt Bev doesn't hold what happened with Rosemarie against him. But after the crap with John going with Travis the night he was killed, it did bring up some of the old emotions. Aunt Bev was worried she had lost her only living child that night. Now if only we could get Tad to give up the ghost."

"Maybe mating will help."

"If anyone can do it, then Courtney and Milo can. We should get some sleep, tomorrow I want to put together a plan to keep Ivy safe and see what we can do to find her brother." Turi stepped away from the banister and looked at his brother. The resentment of always having to deal with sleuth business while Trey did his own thing was nearly gone. Maybe the mating was going to fix things completely between them.

I can only hope.

Chapter Nine

Ivy woke with fear icing her veins. Something had hauled her out of a deep sleep. She glanced around the dark room and found nothing. Too terrified to move, she lay there listening, waiting for something or someone to attack. Convinced Randolph or his men had come back for her, she couldn't breathe.

Scooting up in bed, she pressed her back against the beautifully carved wood headboard and wished for some of Chad's courage. He wouldn't stay in bed scared of whatever went bump in the night; he'd face it head-on, even if it meant his death.

"At least then I'll die on my own terms and with courage." She could hear his voice in her head as if he was right beside her, repeating the line he had told her numerous times.

Chad might have jumped out of bed, ready to take on whatever was waiting, but he had two key things she didn't—the ability to shift and a gun. She glanced to the nightstand checking for anything she could use as a weapon. Her gaze quickly passed over the alarm clock, her cell phone, and finally settled on the only thing she could use: the lamp. It wasn't much against a shifter, but it was all she had.

Her fingers wrapped around the base of the lamp and a sense of freedom poured through her. She'd used the lamp to stand her ground, and as long as she didn't beg at the end, she would die with a little dignity.

"Ivy..." A deep voice whispered from the hallway.

Was it Trey or Turi? She could feel them nearby, but without the mating complete, she couldn't tell where they were except in the house. She almost replied, but she feared it was someone else and her throat went dry.

A dominating figured stepped into the door frame, filling it almost completely. "Are you okay?"

With the compassion in his voice and the spicy aroma of his beast drifting toward her, she recognized him even though she couldn't see his face across the dark room. "Trey!" She dropped the lamp and reached out to him.

"Angel, I didn't mean to scare you." He crossed the room and wrapped his arms around her.

"It's not you, I'm jumpy." She whispered against his chest, her hands sliding up his back, pulling him closer.

"You're safe here." He massaged her back in small circles, soothing her. "There's nothing to worry about."

"Where's Turi?" Before she'd fallen asleep, she had learned it was Turi's house and that Trey lived next door. Yet it was Trey who came to her in the middle of the night.

"He's down talking to Dad and my brothers." She pulled back from him, the fear returning. "*Shhh*, angel. Everything is fine. I know you're concerned with anyone knowing your heritage…"

"Please, if you tell anyone it will put all of us in danger." Her heart pounded as a cold sweat crawled along her spine.

He rubbed his hand along her back, but his attempt to soothe her wasn't working; the fear wouldn't be pushed aside so easily.

"My brothers and I have been on the front lines of this war against the rogues, we'll be up against Randolph and his men, and they need to know *everything* that could play into the fight. Going in unprepared could get any of us killed. If he knows about you, then he'll try to use it to his advantage, but if they already know your heritage Randolph no longer has the upper hand."

"But if he doesn't know and this spreads…"

"It will go no further than those who can help. They're going to find out if Ty knows."

She pulled out of his embrace. "I told you only Chad and Mason knows."

"As Queen of the Tigers, Tabitha is able to access information without being told. She's connected to any clan who has vowed their loyalty. It's possible she could have felt it through Mason's connection to her. If not, there is also the book."

"Book?"

"It's a magical book that has been handed down through her family for generations. It has been her step-by-step guide, and has helped whenever she needed it. They knew Alaskan Tigers'

Lieutenant Raja had to find his mate before things could be set into motion, and they even knew who it would be. The book gave them all the information."

"So they might know." She pulled her legs up against her chest. "This is all getting so out of hand. It was supposed to be kept quiet, only Chad and Mason would ever know. I had mixed feelings about even telling my mate, if I even found one. When I found you and Turi I knew the truth had to be told. I never expected so many people to find out."

"It's overwhelming now, but we're going to see that everything works out. Randolph will be no threat to you, I promise."

"How much danger will everyone else be in though?"

"No more than they have been." Tentatively he reached out to her and placed his hand on her knee. "Don't worry, nothing's going to happen to us. We're trained to deal with this type of situation from an early age. Everything is going to be fine and we're going to make sure you're safe."

She laid her hand over his, interlocking their fingers. "How's Turi handing things?"

"You mean having to share his new mate with his idiot brother or the news of her heritage?"

"Everything, and you're not the idiot brother. The two of you just have different personalities. There's nothing wrong with that. Actually, I think it's pretty amazing you're not carbon copies of each other."

"He's fine. After you fell asleep, we had the first civil conversation we had in a long time. There's no denying the mating desire so we'll have to work out our issues. Hopefully in time he'll trust me." He squeezed her hand. "I'm really not as bad as he makes me out to be."

"I never thought you were." She reached out with her free hand and cupped his cheek, feeling the stubble along his jawline before caressing down to his chin with her thumb.

"When I'm needed I've always been there. Never once have I skirted my duties."

"You're too defensive." She continued to caress his face, her thoughts turning to how his lips would feel against hers. "I can feel you within me, unlike anything I've ever felt before. You're playful and full of life, but you'd never ignore a call from anyone in need."

He tipped his head and kissed her palm. "That scares you, doesn't it?"

"I'd be lying if I said it didn't. However, I wouldn't change this mating either. It sounds strange but I can feel the type of person you are and I'm glad you're my mate." She paused, enjoying his warm breath against her hand. "It's the same with Turi. I can feel him within me, the strong, business side, always in control, and the same desire courses through me for him. I think we've been mated together because we're each part of what the other needs, like three parts of a whole. When we come together we'll make an unstoppable team."

"I don't like the sound of unstoppable, it implies we'll be in a lot of danger. You're human and I want you safe…no danger for you." He kissed the curve of her hand again, this time drawing a fingertip within his mouth and gently sucking it.

"Human, yes…but I do have some shifter blood running within me. Not that it matters, we're living in a dangerous time. There's nothing we can do about that. Instead we just have to protect each other and cherish each day." She leaned forward, advancing on him, until her face was hovering next to his. Her fear had been replaced with a different feeling—but it was just as intense. "Let's cherish this moment."

Chapter Ten

With increasing ardor, Ivy pressed her lips to Trey's. Diving her tongue between his lips, she was met with the spiciness of cinnamon and honey. The taste of him drew her in, wanting more until she was straddling his waist. Her tongue danced around his until she sucked his bottom lip between her teeth, and nipped gently.

"I want you."

"Turi…" Hesitation and need edged his mumbling, while his hands slid under her tank top.

"He'll come to us." She wasn't sure how she knew it, but she could feel him. In her mind, she could see him at a table with some of the men from the party; they were in a kitchen she didn't recognize. Midsentence he glanced up as if he was seeing her. The confusion knitted his brow before he made his excuses.

"We should wait," Trey whispered as he kissed along the nape of her neck.

"He's coming."

"How do you know?"

"I can see him in my mind. He was with men—your brothers I think—but he left and is coming to us. He's coming up the hill now." She tugged his shirt over his head and quickly returned to sliding her fingers along the contours of his chest. "Don't stop."

"You couldn't shut me down with a bunch of angry bears." He pulled the tank top over her head and tossed it to the floor, revealing her naked breasts. The cool air swooshed over her, and her nipples hardened into little buds. He shot her a smirk and lowered his head to claim one of her nipples. Sucking it between his lips, he let his teeth graze over it.

The passion running through her veins had taken control, forcing her to speed the pace. She wanted him. *Needed* was a better way to describe the desire tearing through her. It didn't give her a moment to think this would cement the mating, become the foundation of their life together. Nor did it allow her to pause and wait for Turi, who should be there with them as their mating was taken to the next level.

She pulled the zipper of his jeans down and slipped her hand between the rough material and warm skin. His already growing shaft met her hand, and she wrapped her fingers around it. "Looks like someone's ready." Teasingly she drew her nails down the length. Her body craved his touch, to feel his hands running over her skin.

"I'll always be ready for you." He kissed a path down her neck, letting his warm breath caress her skin. Sensations collided and threatened to overwhelm her when he teased her nipples.

"You two couldn't wait until after I met with the family?" Turi bitched as he stepped into the bedroom.

Trey let her nipple slip from his lips, his mouth hovering just over it. "You didn't have to come. I wouldn't have complained about having her all to myself."

"The way she called to me, I couldn't deny it. How did you do that?" Turi came to stand next to the bed.

"I don't know, it just happened." She reached out. "Join us."

Turi pulled off his shirt and tossed it at the edge of the huge bed. "Do you like what you see?" He teased when her gaze traveled over his chest.

"Oh yes!" She nodded, wanting to run her hands over his chest. Where Trey was toned, Turi was beyond that; his body was carved out of stone, every muscle well defined. There wasn't an ounce of fat on either of the brothers, making her feel little self-conscious. "Come to me."

He unzipped his jeans and let them fall to the floor, his rock hard shaft straining against the thin material of his boxers, which he promptly tugged off. With a heated gaze, he joined them on the bed, nestling himself on the opposite side of Ivy. With torturous slowness, he slid an arm around her waist just above the waistband of her shorts. "I felt that moment of doubt, but there's no need for it. You're gorgeous." He claimed her mouth.

She moaned around Turi's unrelenting kiss, while Trey skimmed her shorts down her legs. He was taking his time, as if unwrapping a present. "We want you naked."

Turi broke the kiss and nodded in agreement. "Always naked."

"I'm not sure about *always*, after all there's life outside the bedroom." She teased before giving a playful tug to Trey's jeans. "Off with these."

He slipped out of them, discarding his boxers while he was at it. "Is this better, angel?"

"Much." She leaned her head back against the pillow and looked from Turi to Trey. "How will this work?"

The men exchanged a glance before Trey asked. "Are you a…"

"Virgin?" When he nodded, she continued. "No. I had a relationship with another human but it was unsatisfying, and there were too many secrets I had to keep from him. It didn't work. I only asked because I've never done it with two…" She stopped, unable to finish the sentence.

"Let us do all the work," Turi whispered, his mouth on her earlobe, gently tugging it with his teeth.

"Claim me." She reached out, her hand landing firmly on Turi's chest, until he lowered closer into her. His shaft pressed tight against her thigh. They had her captive between their bodies, making her feel safe and wanted. In that moment all her fears were gone.

Turi's fingers slid between her legs and teased her bundle of nerves, dragging pleasure from her in hard, hot waves. Trey's fingers caressed along the curve of her hip, his mouth on hers, devouring her. She moaned around his unrelenting kiss, her fingers reaching up to cup the back of his head, keeping him here. While Turi's fingers thrust into her as his thumb continued to wring more pleasure from her core. It took everything in her not to break away from Trey's lips and scream as desire rushed forward with her release on its heels.

"Not yet," Turi whispered, withdrawing his fingers.

Trey's teeth grazed her lower lip and he pulled back enough to let her cries of frustration escape. His fingers caressed every inch of her body, sending moans of ecstasy from her lips. For such a big man, he was incredibly tender, as though trying to memorize every curve of her body with his hands and mouth.

Heat soared through her blood, impatient and demanding. It had been too long since she had been intimate with another, and she wanted them hard and fast. "I need one of you inside me. Now!"

Turi fingers gently eased her legs open farther, giving him just enough room to position himself between them. He slipped on top of her, his bulky frame hovering above her as he stared down at her, desire burning in his eyes. His shaft teased along her entrance without entering as he watched her.

"Turi!" She reached up and grabbed his hips, determined to have him within her.

As if calling his name tore away the last shred of control he had, he drove into her with one powerful thrust. With it came a moan of both pleasure and pain. Even with the foreplay she was still tight, her body wasn't ready for hard and fast yet, but he'd get her there. He gave her no time to catch her breath before he began rocking in and out, slow enough not to cause pain.

She could feel the cord that reined in Trey's desperation to touch her fraying. He pushed her arms above her head, his mouth claiming hers as Turi's pace quickened. She arched her hips into Trey until he cupped her bottom, giving him a deeper angle as he rocked deep within her.

With each pump his hips increased speed, driving the force deeper and faster. Finding a perfect rhythm, their bodies rocked back and forth, tension stretching her tighter as she fought for the release she longed for. Upon that release, she dug her nails into his back, arching her body into his. He pumped twice more and shouted her name as they came together.

Without giving her time to recover, the brothers changed places. Trey slid between her legs, his hands on her hips. "Open your eyes. I want to look into them as I take you for the first time."

As soon as she opened her eyes, he slid deep within her, and she moaned. He filled her slowly, inch by inch. Halfway in, he slid out before thrusting back in, filling her completely with his manhood. His strokes fed her fire like tinder set to dynamite. She reached out until her hand felt along the perfect contours of Turi's chest where he lay beside her. With Trey between her legs, Turi nibbled her neck, his hand cupping her breast until his thumb found her nipple.

Trey set his own tempo, not to be outdone by Turi. Taking it slower, making each stroke count. Her fingers dug into his back, clawing at him as a second orgasm neared. Her body clenched around his erection, sparking the fire within him and sending him pushing deeper and faster into her. His mouth claimed her nipple, pulling the bud between his teeth and applying just the perfect amount of pain to make it pleasurable. As if knowing she was close to a climax Trey sped his pace, slamming into her until their hips hit off each other.

"Trey!" She cried as her orgasm tore through her. Her nails clawed at his back as she pulled herself tight against him, meeting his thrusts. He pumped twice more and shouted her name, his own climax finding him. Eternity stretched on until he collapsed beside her.

Her breath slowly returned to normal and she lay cradled between them. Now that the act had been completed, the mating energy was pouring through them. Connecting them through their thoughts and needs. She could feel them as if they were extensions to her own body.

She finally felt like she belonged somewhere. She belonged with them, in their arms.

Bearing Secrets: Alaskan Tigers

Chapter Eleven

The sun peeked around the edges of the curtains, casting little rays of light dancing about the room. Not wanting to get up, Trey snuggled deeper into bed, his arm tight around Ivy's waist, his head buried in her hair. His bear was content and had no desire to move anytime soon. This was what life was all about; these moments were what they fought for every time they went out on a mission. Turi might doubt their goals, but for Trey, finding his mate had reaffirmed everything. He wanted to make a safer world for her.

With the future in mind, he decided to slip out of bed and take Turi's place with the morning check on the sleuth. It would be one step to proving he was fully committed to their mating and the sleuth. He slipped into his jeans and grabbed his shirt from the bedpost before sneaking out of the room without waking either of them.

Strolling out of the house, he tugged his shirt over his head, and squinted in the sun as his eyes adjusted to the brightness. He tipped his head back to the sky and let the morning breeze coming off the water wake him up. The gentle swoosh of the waves as they hit the beach, the crisp salty air—it was home. For the first time he wondered if they'd be able to convince Ivy to stay on the island if Chad resurfaced. The older Brown brothers might have left, but he had no plans to.

"Trey…" His father called out as he neared his parents' house, where he was sitting on the porch.

"Morning, Dad."

"What has you up this early? Ma mentioned you and Turi found your mate. I figured you boys would be spending a late morning with her."

He climbed the steps and took a seat in one of the handcrafted rocking chairs that lined the porch. "They're still sleep. I thought I'd check on sleuth and see if there was anything you needed dealt with."

"It's been a quiet morning. Everyone is still recovering from the party last night. Even your brothers are still in bed." Devon yawned. "That's where I'd be if it wasn't for your mother up baking all those sweets you boys love so dearly."

"Bears and their sweet tooth," Trey joked, though it was true.

"You boys are worse than any bear I know." Devon brought the mug of coffee to his lips, taking a deep gulp. "Ma tells me your mate is part of the Arizona Tigers. I didn't think they had any *humans* in their ranks."

In spite of himself, Trey laughed, sincerely amused at the way his father stretched *human* out, not as if it was a bad thing, but it was his way of asking for Ivy's story without actually asking. "Turi didn't tell you last night?"

"He only said she needed a safe place, he was about to explain something when he started to stare into space. Next thing I know he's rushing back to his cabin."

"Shit!" Trey rubbed his sweaty palms over his jeans. This should have been coming from Turi; he was the diplomat twin and could smooth out any problems before they had a chance to arise. Without Turi here, Trey took a deep breath and dove in. "She's Randolph's niece."

"What?" His father set the coffee mug aside and looked at him with concern.

Over the next few minutes he explained everything. Hoping to avoid dealing with the same anger Turi originally had when he found out Ivy's heritage, Trey went over her commitment to the tigers in as much detail as he could. He wanted his father to accept her, without wondering if she was going to bring danger to the island.

"Dad…" He paused for a moment, deciding how best to approach it. "We've decided that we only want the immediate family to know. Mom, our brothers, and you. Otherwise it puts her in too much danger."

"So that's why Turi gathered us last night after the celebration." He took another long drink of coffee. "I should beat his ass for gathering us and then disappearing. We had a long day getting everything ready for the party, then the actual party on top of it."

"Dad, the mating desire called him to us. You know how strong that is, he couldn't have stopped himself if he wanted to."

"We'll tell everyone after brunch."

Gazing out at the water in the direction of inland Nome, Trey gently rocked the chair. He hadn't noticed the tension in his shoulders until now, which had grown worse as he waited for his father's approval. "You're okay with all this?"

He nodded. "Mating is a powerful thing, and one of the benefits is you'd know if there was something dangerous about her connection. If you trust her, we will. Plus, Ty wouldn't have brought her here if she was a danger to us."

"But Randolph is."

"That's nothing new and not something she's brought to us. Randolph's been a threat since he took over Pierce's gang of rogues."

He still couldn't believe his sweet mate was related to such a menace. He couldn't understand how someone could turn against their family and their kind. To him that bond was nearly as strong as the one he shared with his mate and twin. That train of thought quickly had him thinking of his dead brother, Travis. It didn't matter how someone was raised, or the family blood that coursed through their veins, some people were just evil. They took pleasure out of seeing others suffer, and joy out of the chase or kill.

"Son…" Devon pulled Trey from his thoughts.

"Yeah."

"I know you and Turi haven't seen eye to eye, and that's going to make challenges within your mating if you're not careful, but you boys can be just as happy as Taber and Thorben."

Trey gave a little chuckle. "Those two nearly killed each other when Taber found out he had to share his mate."

"They overcame, and so will you. I just hope you two stay on the island. It's nice having help with the sleuth." Devon stood. "You did well last night, keeping things smooth with Bev and Tad."

"Thanks, Dad. Tad needs to deal with his guilt."

"We've all been saying that for years, but I think Courtney is finally getting through to him. Who knows? Maybe this trip will allow him to bury his remorse before he goes back to the Alaskan Tigers' compound." Devon stepped around the rockers and opened the door, pausing before he went inside. "Now go back to your mates."

With the sleuth quiet, Trey decided his dad was right. He stood and headed back. He'd balance this new sleuth responsibility and his mates, but right now Ivy's naked body was calling to him.

Bearing Secrets: Alaskan Tigers

Chapter Twelve

Ivy woke to heart-pounding terror, reaching out to where Trey should have been. Her thoughts immediately jumped to Randolph. Had he found them? Terrified, her body went rigid. Everything she'd gone through was finally taking its toll, and even knowing she was overreacting she couldn't calm herself.

"*Shhh...*" Turi whispered, his voice full of sleep. "You're okay."

As if his voice reset the circuits in her brain, she reached out to him. "Where's Trey?" She couldn't keep the fear out of her voice. Had he left her or had something awful happened while she slept?

"I'm right here." She glanced up to find Trey coming through the bedroom door. "Everything is fine. I only went to check on the sleuth."

"Come here." She reached out, needing to feel him, to know he was all right.

He kicked off his shoes and slipped onto the bed. "I didn't mean to worry you." He snuggled up against her, wrapping his arm around her waist.

"It's okay. I just thought something was wrong." Snuggled between their bodies she felt safe and loved. "Can we just stay like this?"

"For as long as you want," Turi whispered and kissed her forehead.

"Not too long," she amended, sighing with contentment now that the mating connection had been reestablished. Now that she was more awake, reality intruded on her thoughts. "Remember, I want a laptop so I can get back to work."

"What is it you're working on, my angel?" Trey kissed along her shoulder, working his way to the nape of her neck.

"Before my life got tossed in a blender on high, I was putting together a proposal of why there should be a group of shifters banding together to keep law and order."

Turi smoothed her hair out of her face. "What is your reasoning behind it?"

"An organization like this will make sure that what happened in Ohio and Texas does not happen again." She rubbed her hand along his naked hip. "I'm sure there're other things I don't know that are happening that should be stopped."

"My sweet angel thinks having a bunch of shifter cops is going to stop it." Trey nibbled her neck.

She couldn't figure out if he was impressed or just thought she was crazy. Either way, it was her project and she was putting it together with or without their support. Someone had to agree with her. "What I think is people need to be saved."

"You think people are just going to talk about what is happening to them?" Turi leaned up on his elbow and looked down at her. "The clan members who were suffering weren't screaming for help. We only found out about Texas because Adam brought Tex back to Alaska after an attack on them."

"Who would be in charge of these…police?" Turi questioned.

"Why not Tabitha? As we speak, she's gaining control over the tigers and eventually she'll control other shifters. She's the perfect choice."

"You think the other shifter groups that aren't tigers are going to be willing to have her as the complete ruler?" Turi's hand paused on her cheek.

"I know it would be hard, but something needs to be done. If we're going to live among humans, we need to control ourselves, that means we need *one* organization to keep everyone in line. Tabitha is that person, but she needs people to go out and enforce it."

"I like how you think." Trey nuzzled against her. "Turi, that's along the same lines as why I wanted to do the forum."

She rolled onto her back enough that she could look at Trey who lay behind her. "Forum?"

"About a year ago, Turi and I discussed starting an online forum. It would be buried deep enough that humans wouldn't be able to find it, but it would be a place for shifters to be able to socialize, get help with their problems, and we'd be able to monitor it for any crimes being committed against our kind."

"That's a marvelous idea, why don't you do it? I could add it into my proposal as another way of monitoring things."

"She's right about the forum." Turi nodded. "After you two fell asleep last night I started thinking about it. We could make a difference with it, and it could be used to help Tabitha communicate with the other Alphas. The possibilities of the good it could do are endless."

"I'd like to help in any way I can." She took their hands in hers. "We'll make a good team."

"We already are." Turi tipped his head toward Trey. "You've reminded me that though Trey and I are twins we're different people. Each of us have our own way of dealing with things, and even though I prefer things done my way, he's not half bad. We each have our strengths and that's what we need to focus on."

Trey glanced at her before looking back at his brother. "What are you saying?"

"Help with the sleuth as you can and when you're needed but I think you should focus on the forum, and I'll help you with what you need. Each of us playing to our strengths will make us a better team."

"Are you sure?" The surprise was clear in Trey's voice.

"Yes." Turi leaned down and kissed Ivy's forehead. "Later I want you to finish the proposal. My laptop is in my office. Feel free to use it, and if I can be of any assistance let me know."

"You said later, what did you have in mind for now?"

"To stay cuddled with you until we have to go to Mom's for breakfast." He shoved his arm under his pillow and laid his head down. His eyes instantly closed as his head hit the pillow and he snuggled against her. "Better get used to it. Bears love their sleep."

"Don't forget their cuddles." Trey snuggled closer against her, his eyes closing.

"Good thing I enjoy both of those." She closed her eyelids and enjoyed the moment. The rest of the world and worries would have to wait. Right now, all she wanted to do was appreciate the two men she was destined to spend forever with. *My mates.*

Bearing Secrets: Alaskan Tigers

Chapter Thirteen

Curled up on the sofa with a roaring fire and the laptop, Ivy couldn't focus. She had been on the island for over twenty-four hours and received no word from Ty. She glared at her cell phone, willing it to ring, but nothing happened. It had been three days since the attack on the Arizona compound and not a word from Chad. He had to be dead. It pained her to think it, but what other reason could there be?

She rolled her shoulders and tried to put it out of her mind. The proposal was open in front of her, with a completely new section to include the forum Trey was going to start, but she couldn't focus. Instead, she set the laptop aside and leaned back, resting her head against the sofa.

Why worry when there's nothing I can do? Not for the first time, she wished she was a shifter. Then she could be out there looking for Chad, Mason, and anyone else who might have survived the attack. She hated sitting there feeling useless.

The front door swung open, and suspecting it to be Turi returning, Ivy called out. "I'm in here."

"Good to know." A soft female voice replied.

Ivy spun around to see who it was and recognized the two women from the celebration. They'd been sitting on either side of the tiger who had shifted his hand and scratched Trey's butt after the lap dance. "Umm…Turi's out at the moment and Trey's getting a shower."

"No worries, we came to see you. Can we come in?" The same woman spoke, both of them still standing in the doorway. Each with a bottle of wine and glasses.

Ivy knew they had to play into the Brown family somehow, she just wasn't sure how. "Umm, sure. You're related somehow, right?"

"I'm Courtney, Tad and Milo's mate." She tipped her head to the side, sending her long auburn hair spilling into her face. "That's Kallie."

"I'm mated to the first set of Brown twins, Taber and Thorben." Kallie came around the sofa, and Ivy was unable to tear her gaze away from the white streaks in Kallie's brown hair.

When she realized Kallie had caught her staring she quickly looked away. "I'm sorry."

"Don't be. I'm used to it."

"It was rude, and we're family now." Ivy tugged her legs under her to make room. "Please sit, make yourselves comfortable."

"The stripes are from the years I spent locked in my tigress form," Kallie explained, taking the seat next to Ivy.

"I know…" Ivy shook her head and tried not to sound like an idiot. "I mean there was a young man in the Arizona Tigers who had the same thing. I didn't stare because I was in shock, or because I didn't know what caused it, but because I was amazed at how striking it is. Women pay hundreds of dollars to have highlights done and to dye their hair crazy colors, but even the best stylist couldn't do what's natural on you."

"I guess it's like the women with curly hair who spend hours trying to straighten it while those with straight hair try to make it curly." Kallie smirked. "I've spent years trying to get rid of them, but no hair coloring hides them. It wasn't until I met my mates that I accepted them."

"Enough about that." Courtney handed each of them a glass of wine. "We came to welcome you to the family. It's nice to see another human in the mix of shifters."

"I thought you might want some tricks on dealing with twins when it comes to mating. I know mine are a handful." Kallie let out a light laugh and it was hard not to join in. "With that being said, I wouldn't change Taber and Thorben for the world. They are my rock. Grumpy at times, but don't we all have moments like that?"

"I think bears are grumpier than most." Courtney smirked over her wine glass. "I should know, I have a tiger and a bear. Some days I feel like I should be a punch line of some joke, a bear, a tiger, and a human walk into a bar…"

"What's going on here?" Trey stood in the hallway with only a towel wrapped around his waist.

"Go put some clothes on," Kallie ordered. "Your brothers would have your ass for being that naked around us women, especially after last night."

"I was only trying to lighten the mood and now I have the claw marks for my trouble." He glared at Courtney.

"My mate has always been a little quick to draw his claws." Courtney gave a light chuckle as if she was thinking of something else he used those claws for. "We only stopped by to welcome her to the family. You know, and share all those hidden Brown secrets."

"Like how we keep you in line," Kallie shouted after him as he turned to go back to the bedroom. "You've got to keep them in line or they'll order you around day and night."

Courtney nodded in agreement. "They're protective, which is something I had to get used to since I didn't even know about shifters until they showed up in my life."

"I know how they can be. I can only image what my brother would have to say if he knew I was mated to bears." Ivy laughed at the thought, before tears glistened in her eyes.

"I'm sorry." Courtney laid a hand on Ivy's knee. "We don't know anything yet. Don't give up hope."

"It's so unlike him…we're close, he should have contacted me." She wiped away the tears before they could fall.

"He'd have to get the Alpha to safety." Kallie reassured Ivy.

"I'm sorry, but I'm tired of hearing that. He could have sent me a quick text message or called, just so I'd know he was okay. Our cell phones are untraceable. There's no excuse why he couldn't…" She trailed off unable to finish the thought.

"Ivy…" Courtney squeezed her thigh. "He could have lost his phone in the attack. Ty has a team out searching for him. They'll find him. I know it's hard but right now all you can do it wait."

"Sorry." Ivy wiped away her tears and took a deep breath. "You girls came over here and I'm such a downer."

"We're family through thick and thin. Right how it's hard, but never doubt we're all behind you." Kallie set her wine glass aside. "You'll get through this, we'll see to it."

"Thank you." Ivy forced herself to smile. It was nice having them there, and to be part of a bigger family. She especially liked the idea of having sisters, having someone she could confide in. Though she and Chad were close, there were things she couldn't discuss with him.

"So tell me, how are you dealing with the idea of being mated to twins?" Kallie inquired.

"It's…I don't know…surprising and amazing." She took a sip of the wine and thought about Turi and Trey. "They're identical in appearance but that's it. In every other aspect, they're completely different. Each of them with their own personality, wants, needs, and desires. It seems overwhelming."

"Oh, I understand that." Kallie's lips curled up into a smile. "Mine are a little more alike in personality, wants, and needs, but it can totally be overwhelming at times. Though I wouldn't change it for a moment."

"Last night was amazing, but now that the mating has been complete and I can feel them within me, it's almost too much." Ivy couldn't believe she just hinted at her sex life to two women who were practically strangers.

"The mating connects your emotions allowing you to—" Kallie started to explain.

"I know that, but I mean it's more than that." Ivy sipped her wine and took a moment to find the right words. "It's not just their emotions, I can *feel* them. I know where they are, what they are doing. It's like I can see them in my mind. Last night, Turi was down at his parents, when things…started. I could see him get up from the table and come to us."

"You were calling to him." Kallie took a sip from her wine. "I've heard only Alphas and their mates can do that without having to focus. Everyone else has to hone that skill and really focus on their mate. Even then it's just bits and pieces, unless you're like Ty and Tabitha."

"Their thoughts…it's like they're my own."

Kallie turned on the sofa so she could face Ivy completely. "Now that's unusual and, I'm sure, unnerving. Do they have yours?"

"I asked them this morning, they said not always but it's like only when I want them to."

"Now that could be fun, especially in the bedroom." Courtney giggled. "Think…you'll always get it how you want it."

"That's how I realized it." Ivy felt her cheeks heat, but she forced herself to continue. "You know how you think *a little harder,* or *a little to the right*, well they knew just that and, oh boy, was it amazing."

"Color me jealous," Courtney announced, scooting to the edge of the chair. "Think of all the fun you could have with that."

"Right now I'm not sure the fun wins out. It's maddening to have two additional trains of thoughts running through my head."

"I guess it would have some drawbacks." Kallie laid her hand over Ivy's. "When Robin was suffering with something similar, Ty was able to give her some helpful tips on how to separate them. Maybe they'd work for you."

"Robin? Isn't that Adam's mate? I think he said something about her during the helicopter ride here."

"Yeah, she's human but when Harmony—who is mated to Felix the Captain of Tabitha's guards—joined our clan she formed an Alpha-shifter connection with Robin. It was nearly overwhelming to Robin with all the pain." Kallie explained. "They still have the connection, even though Harmony's committed to the Alaskan Tigers. It's unheard of to have it with a human, let alone still have the connection once committed to an Alpha and mated."

"Maybe I'll see if Turi or Trey will contact him for me, then I can see if there's any news on Chad."

"I know my Alpha. He'd call if there was any news." Kallie squeezed her hand.

That's what Ivy was afraid of. She glanced at her cell phone again, begging it to ring.

Bearing Secrets: Alaskan Tigers

Chapter Fourteen

Need and desire coursed through Turi's veins, speeding his steps until he was jogging. This mating had him doing things he'd never done before, like leaving sleuth duties until later. Right now, all he could think about was getting his mate naked, it had his shaft rock hard and his bear on edge. It wouldn't be denied any longer.

With a twist of the handle he opened the door and instantly smelled his sister-in-laws. "My sweet mate, I'm back."

"In here."

Ivy's tears permeated the air, making him want to go to her. What had Kallie and Courtney said to her? "What's going on here?" Suspicious, he raised an eyebrow.

"Kallie and Courtney came to let me in on all those Brown secrets you've been hiding."

"I thought family stuck together, hiding our dirt," he joked, eyeing the women.

"She's family now, so it's time to let all those skeletons out of the closet. Just think, she's already mated to you and Trey so there's no running now. We could have done it last night," Courtney joked, as if that would have stopped the mating.

"I tried to stop them, but they kicked me out." Trey came down the hallway to where everyone was gathered.

"We sent you to get dressed." Kallie tossed a throw pillow at him, which he caught midair.

"Oh, Trey." He shot a glance to his twin. "Tell me you didn't stroll through my house naked with everyone out there."

"Give me some credit, I had a towel on."

"One that did nothing to hide his desire." Courtney's comment got the throw pillow tossed back at her, but unlike Trey, she wasn't ready for it and it hit her on the top of her head. "You'll pay for that, *bear*. I'll get Milo on you again."

"Come on, Courtney. It's obvious the mates would like to be alone." Kallie rose from the sofa. "We'll be here on the island for a little bit longer, if you want to chat more."

"Thanks," Ivy said softly as they made their way to the door.

"Umm…wonder what we can do now." Trey came around the sofa and advanced on her.

"Don't even think about it, brother." Turi shut the door, and came to stand behind her. "I have plans for our mate and that involves a shower with me."

"I've already showered," Trey complained.

"Who invited you? I left you alone here with her, you could have done whatever you pleased." He slipped his hand into hers. "Would you join me?"

"In his defense, I was trying to work on the proposal." She squeezed his hand.

"He can have you next. Now I need a shower and I'd like you to join me if you can tear yourself away from your work for a bit."

"Go ahead, angel," Trey encouraged. "I won't be long behind, be sure of that."

Turi tugged her toward the master bedroom. He couldn't stop; he needed to get her naked. Images of her in the shower with the water cascading onto her smooth skin had been haunting him all day. His bear clawed at him, demanding his mate.

Closing the bedroom door behind them, he pulled her into his arms, tight against his chest. "Oh, my sweet mate, I've missed you."

"You were only gone an hour." She slid her hands under his shirt, tugging it out of the waist of his jeans, her fingers raked up his back. "I thought you had more in mind than just a cuddle session."

"Oh, I do." He nibbled along the curve of her neck, before finding the little hollow behind her earlobe. He sunk his teeth into it until he applied just enough pressure to feel her stiffen under his fingers. He eased back and let his tongue tease over the tender flesh, before he drew a deep breath, inhaling her sweet scent. "I love how you respond to the simplest of my touches," he murmured against her neck.

"Don't get cocky, I only want your body." She teased and unbuttoned his jeans. "Now get out of your clothes, I like you without them."

He pulled off his shirt and tossed it to the floor. "I'll get the shower started. Join me once you done." He strolled toward the bathroom, knowing she'd be unwilling to wait idly while he showered. There was no doubt she'd strip and follow him.

In the bathroom, he stripped off the rest of his clothes, tossing them in the laundry basket, and turned toward the large shower. This was another one of his favorite aspects because the shower was large enough for an orgy of bears, and lined the whole back wall. The glass mosaic titles of blues and greens lined the walls, but the best part was the rain showerheads that covered almost every inch of the top, making sure that no matter where someone stood they'd be under the water.

He pulled open the glass door and turned the handle. Steam instantly began billowing out, filling the bathroom. The heat of the water called to his tight muscles; he wanted it as much as he wanted her.

* * *

Ivy stripped off her clothes as quickly as she could, and tossed them on the cedar chest at the bottom of the huge bed. Cool air blew across her nipples as she padded toward the bathroom, following one of the men she couldn't get off her mind.

She slipped into the shower without waiting for an invitation. Turi stood with his back to her under the raining showerheads, soap running down his body. Even though he didn't turn around, his back muscles tightened. For a moment, she stood there enjoying the way the soap bubbles slid over his body. Giving into her temptation, she ran her hands up his slippery back.

"I knew you'd join me." He leaned back letting the water run through his hair and forcing it away from his face.

"Wow." She glanced around the bathroom. "You guys had me so out of it last night I didn't even notice the shower when I got ready for bed."

"I like that we have you so off your game that you miss things." He advanced on her and pushed her against the cool title, grasping her wrists with one hand and holding them hostage above her head.

"This need within me for you two keeps me off my game. All I can think about is you and Trey." She leaned forward, wanting him to kiss her. "It's more than the fact that you've invaded every thought I have. You keep my body on edge."

"Let me take the edge off you." He crushed his mouth to hers, and slid his hand between her legs. Unerringly finding her core, his fingers found her nub, working his thumb and forefinger to drive the pleasure from her. His thumb slid over the nerve endings until heat erupted against his touch radiating in tingling waves outward, weakening her legs. If he hadn't been bracing her against the wall, she'd have slid down onto the floor. Fierce desire rose within her like a tidal wave smashing through a dam.

"Take me," she murmured against his mouth, holding onto him as wild delight streamed through her.

His teeth grazed her lower lip and he pulled his hand away. She cried out in frustration, but he ignored her demands. Gripping her hips, he lifted her and spread her thighs before he drove into her with one powerful thrust. Ivy moaned and twined her arms around his shoulders as he withdrew and thrust into her again, deeper, harder, his pumping almost savage as he revealed some of the beast within. The water pummeled from the outside while his pounding sparked sensations inside of her she'd never experienced.

She had no control, no say, as he left her mouth, and kissed a path to her neck. Digging her nails into his shoulders, she held on as every pump of his hips sent pulses of pleasure exploding through her. Her legs tightened around him as he groaned and shoved himself deeper into her. The pressure built within her until her body trembled and another orgasm rushed upon her. She held onto him as he slammed home in a frenzy. Her nails digging into his shoulders as a climax tour through her with such force her world came apart at the seams, her inner muscles clenched around him as he continued to drive into her.

This man utterly devastated her. If it wasn't for her legs around his body, she would have collapsed into a heap.

Chapter Fifteen

Timing it perfectly, Trey opened the shower door just as they finished. Hard and ready, he stepped into the shower. Ivy lifted her head from Turi's shoulder, and her gaze traveled over his body. Desire returned to her forest green eyes as Turi slipped out of her.

Trey sat down on the cool stone bench. "Come here."

"What?" she questioned, not moving from her spot against the wall.

"I want you to ride me." He held out a hand to her and raised an eyebrow when she still didn't move. "Don't make me come get you."

"Cat and mouse games shouldn't be played in the shower." She strolled toward him, swaying her hips in a rhythm that almost had him lose his load right there.

"Damn, you're beautiful," he whispered, pulling her into his lap until she was straddling his hard-on. The hot water had turned her skin a rose red, and her nipples hardened with excitement. He lowered his head and placed his lips over one of her nipples. Gently pulling it into his mouth, he let it roll over his tongue, while his hand slid between her legs. He slid his thumb over her nub, and drove his fingers into her.

"Trey…" She dug her nails into his arms. "I need you inside of me."

"I want to make sure you're ready for me." He whispered, watching the passion ignite within her until she was burning like a bonfire.

"Now, Trey…now!" She begged, her body reacting to each pump of his fingers.

He slipped his hand away, moving them to her hips, and gently eased her down onto his shaft. As he slid his full length into her, she arched her back, and let her head fall back against Turi's waiting chest.

"What…" Surprise to find him there filled her voice.

"Just relax, enjoy what Trey's offering, I'm only going to add to the experience." Turi leaned down and began kissing the nape of her neck.

"My angel, look at me." Trey waited until she did. "Your eyes are like the window to your soul, I want them open. I want to *see* what you're feeling, not just feel it within me."

With her eyes open and watching him, he slid his hands over her hips, gliding her down on his shaft, filling her slowly, inch by inch. Halfway in, he forced her body up until he was nearly out of her, before thrusting back in, filling her completely with his manhood.

"Trey!" She cried out when he was completely inside of her. She pressed her body tighter against Turi, who had his arm wrapped around her just under her breast, teasing one of her nipples with his fingers.

With his hands on her hips, Trey increased their pace until she was slamming onto him, driving the force with each pump. The thrusts became deeper and faster, falling into a perfect tempo, moving with such precision. She rode him while the tension stretched within him.

Clawing her nails over his chest, she climaxed around his manhood. His hands quickly grabbed hold of her hips, keeping the pace as she began to flounder, keeping the rhythm strong until his own orgasm followed and he roared her name.

Turi stepped away, turning off the water that had begun to turn cold, while Trey pressed her against his body. "You're amazing."

"I know." She teased.

"A woman who knows her value." Turi wrapped a towel around her shoulders, and helped her stand. "I love it."

"I think we should continue this in the bedroom because I'm not done with you two yet." She ran her hands over their chests.

Trey stood from the bench, and lifted her into his arms. "My angel, that can be arranged." He carried her to the bed, where he laid her in the center before joining her, Turi taking the other side.

"Anything you want from us…" Turi mumbled, finding her nipple with his lips.

"*Anything?*" She rose onto her elbow and glanced at him.

"What's on your mind, my angel?" Trey ran his fingers along her cheek.

"I need a favor."

Both men went still. Trey shared a glance with his brother before looking back at her.

Turi's mouth stopped mid-motion and he let her nipple slip from between his teeth. "I have a feeling what you're about to say is going to ruin the mood."

"From the look on her face, I'd say that's a given," Trey agreed. "What is it?"

"I need to go back to Arizona."

"Absolutely not!" Trey shot out of bed. "We're not going to have you put yourself in danger. You're safe here and that's where you're staying."

"Why?" Turi asked his arm still around her waist.

"You can't be seriously listening to this. We can't risk our mate." Trey growled.

"I want to check the place where Chad and I would go to escape the pressures of the clan when we were growing up. It was our place, the only place I didn't have to hear any of the snide remarks from the children of the clan. I could just be myself." She ran her hand through her wet hair. "If Chad's alive and needed somewhere to go, he might go there. It's a place that only the two of us know about and it's far enough from the clan's land that he'd be safe. It might be the only place he'd go if one of them were injured."

"Then we'll have someone check, because you're not going." Trey stood next to the bed, his arms crossed over his chest, completely naked.

"Don't you understand? I can't sit here and do nothing. If it was your brother you'd be out there looking for him."

"My angel, that's different."

"Why, because I'm not a shifter? Or because I'm a woman?" She pushed out of Turi's embrace and sat up in bed.

"Ivy…" Turi ran his hand down her arm. "He's right, it is too dangerous for you to go. The connection you have with Randolph will put you in more danger. If any of his followers are there, they might be able to smell the connection in your blood. We can't risk it. Instead, tell me where it is and I'll have a team check it out."

"That doesn't change the fact I can't sit here and do nothing. This is killing me." She leaned back against the pillow, her head pressed against the beautiful carvings Theodore had added into the wood. "Trey, I didn't mean to upset you. It's just…I don't know what to do."

"I promise you, Ty and the others are doing everything possible to find Chad and anyone else who might have survived." He came to her, taking her hand in his. "In the meantime let us keep you occupied."

"We're not doing this to stifle you. Our only desire is to keep you safe," Turi chimed in.

"It feels wrong to do nothing."

Trey squeezed her hand. "I don't know Chad but I can't believe he'd want you out there risking yourself, would he?"

"Chad's always been too protective."

"No, he cares about you and so do we. We protect the people we love." Turi met her gaze with one of determination. "As hard as it is to sit by and do nothing, how do you think it would feel for any of us if we let you go off halfcocked after him and something happened?"

"Listen, my sweet angel." Trey dragged his thumb over her knuckles, circling each one with precision. "I have a friend, he's a private investigator and a black panther shifter, I'll call him and see if he can help locate Chad."

"Call Ty first, see if they have any leads. It will give Simon an idea of where to start," Turi told his brother. "On second thought, do you think he'll help us after what just happened?"

"What happened?" She looked between them in confusion.

"It's a long story but Simon's brother, Quinn, is a United States Marshall. Courtney witnessed a high profile murder with some drug runners and a rather nasty man and was in witness protection. Quinn was handling the case. It was going to be a career maker, and it fell apart," Trey explained before grabbing his cell phone from the nightstand.

"On the verge of repeating myself, what happened?"

"The killer was out on bond and came after Courtney. He blew up her house, killing another Marshal, and she ran from Texas to Alaska. It's how Tad and Milo met her, and when the killer followed they were there to protect her. In the end, Tad and Milo killed this guy after he shot my father." With a quick kiss to the top of her hand, he stood up from the bed. "Why don't you try to rest? Turi will stay with you, and I'll go make the call."

Without waiting for an answer, he strolled from the room. He needed to make the call and get someone on the case to ease the turmoil boiling within his mate. Ivy needed to know one way or another what had happened to Chad. If he was killed in the attack she needed to know so she could grieve. If he was alive someone needed to find him. He was going to find those answers for her, even if it meant he had to travel to Arizona himself.

Bearing Secrets: Alaskan Tigers

Chapter Sixteen

Exhaustion clung to Turi, making his movements slow as he entered his parents' house. It seemed as though he had just closed his eyes when he received the call about the meeting. The sun wouldn't be up for hours, which meant one thing, whatever the reason for the gathering, it had to be important.

"Here." His mom handed him a steaming hot mug of coffee.

"Does this mean sleep is out of the question?"

His father glanced up from the paper he was reading. "It shouldn't take long and then you can get some sleep. If you don't want the coffee, set it aside. Your mother needed something to do. Saying goodbye is never easy for her. Sit down, son."

Stifling a yawn, he set the mug aside, and leaned against the armrest of the sofa. If there was a chance he'd be able to go back to bed, he'd wait on the coffee. "What's happening, Dad?"

"On the sofa!" His mom hollered as she made her way back into the kitchen. "You're too big to be sitting on the armrests."

Years of training had told him it was better to do what his mother said than disobey, because she'd find a way to make him pay later. He sank down on the sofa cushion and waited to be filled in.

"Ty called and requested Taber and Milo join the team in Arizona. They're leaving shortly, while Thorben, Kallie, Tad, and Courtney stay behind."

"They found Chad?" Suddenly the doubt that Ivy's brother had survived was replaced with a hint of hope.

"Not yet, but with Ivy's lead you passed on to Ty, and Simon's suggestions there's a few places they need to search. Ty's hopeful. There are some signs, which he didn't get into, but they point to the possibility Chad and at least one other are alive."

"I should go."

Devon shook his head. "No, right now Ivy needs both of her mates. If he's found, we can make arrangements, but until then she needs the comfort you and Trey can give her."

He nodded, knowing that here he could do his best to keep her occupied. "She's having a hard time doing nothing."

"As I'm sure you and Trey are. It's engrained within us to do something to ease our mates suffering." Devon took a drink of his coffee before continuing. "I wanted you to know what was happening, and it's your choice if you wish to tell Ivy."

"Hopefully she'll still be asleep when I get back, so I won't have to worry about that now."

"Don't worry about the sleuth. I want you to stay with her, do your best to keep her mind off things, and when there's an update Ty will call."

"Your dad and I are here if she needs anything. Kallie and Courtney are too if she wants to talk to a younger woman," his mom added as she came back into the room.

"Thanks, Mom." The one thing about a family like his was the support they had for each other. Not all bears lived with such closeness. Some might belong to a sleuth but be spread out, never seeing each other except during specialized events. "I should get back to her."

"What, you're not going to see us off?" Taber stepped inside, the door banging shut behind him.

"Not with a beautiful woman waiting for me." Turi rose from the sofa. "If I was you I'd be on the plane heading out. The sooner you go, the sooner you can get back to Kallie."

"Isn't that the truth? At least with Thorben here I know she'll be watched over. Same with Tad and Courtney." Taber nodded. "I only wanted to let you know we're heading out. I'll inform you if there are any updates."

"Thanks." Turi laid his hand on Taber's shoulder and gave it a little squeeze. "Be safe, and bring my mate's brother back to her."

"I'll do what I can."

Turi couldn't ask for more, nor did he expect anything less from his brother. It wouldn't have mattered who they were going after in Arizona, Taber and the others would do their best to find them.

He walked out of the house, slightly relieved he wasn't going and that he could stay with his mate, while on the other hand disappointed he wouldn't be the one to bring Chad back to her. Though if Chad wasn't alive, he didn't want to be the one to tell her—to admit he failed her.

He shoved his hands in the pockets of his jeans and ambled back toward his cabin. A shooting star streaked through the sky, giving him hope that the mission would go well.

Stop obsessing, everything's going to be fine. We'll make sure of it.

* * *

Ivy wasn't sure what woke her, but she suspected it had been the chill from not having the warmth of her men on either side of her. Sleep just wouldn't return until Turi came to cuddle against her. Instead of lying there, tossing and turning until she woke Trey, she slipped out of bed and padded to the window seat. She gazed into the darkness. Beyond the glass, darkness cloaked the grounds. Tall pines cast deep shadows that should have been menacing but instead seemed to offer comfort. Where had Turi gone at such a late hour? Had something happened within the sleuth?

She wrapped a throw around her, hiding her naked body from view and stared out into the water. Somewhere out in that darkness danger lied in wait for anyone unsuspecting. It was as if now that her life had been touched with evil, from the attack on her clan, she could no longer see the beauty in things. She wondered about the threats that could be lurking in the shadows. The island was a sanctuary, but what happened when she left the safety of being surrounded by water? Would the fear grow stronger? Would she ever be able to live a normal life again?

One thing nagged her the most. Would Randolph find out her relation to him? She had been hidden away on the Arizona Tigers' land; even if he suspected her mother had a child, there was little chance he knew who or where she was. But things had changed. If he went to her home—or what was left of it—there was no doubt he'd pick up on her smell. If he found out who she was, there was no doubt he'd try to use her as a pawn in whatever he was playing at. She wouldn't allow him to screw with her and the people she cared about, no matter the cost.

"What are you doing awake?" Turi whispered through the darkness.

She turned away from the window to find him standing in the doorway. "I woke up to find you gone, and couldn't get back to sleep. Where did you go?"

He drew near, each step tentative as if he was debating something. "Taber and Milo are joining the search in Arizona."

"Is there…" Unable to stop the excitement, she moved off the edge of the window seat.

"Hold on, Ivy." He stopped her before she could stand. "I don't have all the details but it is believed there might be two alive. A team from the Alaskan Tigers is there, heading things up. Jinx has sent some additional men from the West Virginia Tigers and now Taber and Milo will be joining them. We just have to wait."

"Waiting is the hardest thing."

In one quick movement, he sat down next to her and wrapped one arm around her. "I know, love, I know. We're going to find him."

"In what condition?" She forced the words past the lump of emotion that tightened her throat.

"You have to hope for the best. The fact they didn't find him when they searched through the remains of the compound is a good sign."

Trey rolled over, his gaze drilling into them until he let out a growl of annoyance. "Will you two come back to bed or go to another room?"

"Trey's always been grumpy when his sleep is interrupted." Turi smoothed his hand down Ivy's arm. "We're not going to know anything for a few hours. Do you want to lie back down, or go to the living room?"

"Maybe we could find another way to pass the time." She kissed his neck.

"Woman, you'll wear me out," Turi teased.

"Don't even think about it! You're not doing that in this bed while I'm trying to sleep." Trey tapped the bed next to him. "Come to bed, we all need to catch some sleep and in the morning I'll make it up to you. I promise."

"He's right, we do need some rest. Let's go to bed and cuddle." He stood and stripped out of his clothes before holding his hand out to her.

She let him take her hand and lead her to the bed. "Cuddles lead from one thing to another."

Bearing Secrets: Alaskan Tigers

Chapter Seventeen

There was something about knowing there were teams in Arizona looking for Chad that gave Ivy peace of mind, and for the first time she was able to relax enough to work on the proposal. Her fingers flew over the keyboard, adding the different aspects of the forum that Trey had given her into the overall plan. Her thoughts ran with new ideas, demanding she make note of them to come back to later. For the first time since the attack on her clan, she felt like she had her life back and that she was contributing to the betterment of shifters.

As if things were going too well to last, the last words from a clan tigress she'd considered her best friend played out in her mind. *You're not a shifter, why would you even care?* Before she could explain, the compound had erupted with the first explosive attack, sending Edith running from the house in tigress form. She hadn't made it fifty yards before more blasts shook the ground and gunfire had begun.

Loud beeps from the computer forced her attention back to her lap. Without realizing it, her balled fists had struck the laptop causing it to send a series of beeps in warning before freezing.

Damn it. She leaned her head back against the sofa, her chest tightened, the pain was so deep, so agonizing, at the memory of seeing Edith flying through the air, a hole the size of a grapefruit opening her chest. Her heart had been blown from her body, making it impossible for her to heal from the injuries, one of the few ways a shifter could actually be killed.

With a deep breath numbness settled over her. There was nothing she could do for Edith then and nothing to be done now. Ivy grieved for her clan family and hoped the others had understood why she had done the things she did. The ability to shift might not be within her, but that didn't make her any less part of the clan. She had been raised within the clan since she was a baby and was devoted to the Alpha and the clan. The idea that at the time of their deaths, some might have still have doubted her commitment mangled her heart beyond recognition.

"My sweet angel, are you okay?" Trey glanced at her from behind the desk in Turi's office that they had taken over.

With a forced smile, she pushed her thoughts away and turned to him. "Fine, why?"

"I could feel your distress. If you're worried about Chad…"

"I'm not." She tucked a strand of her hair behind her ear. "I was just remembering the attack, and the last words I said to someone I thought was my friend."

"Thought?" Intrigued, he leaned forward.

"A few hours before the attack, a few of the clan members found out I was working on this proposal." She leaned forward on the chaise lounge, placing the laptop on the table beside it. "The people I thought were my friends, my family…for the first time I saw distrust in their eyes. None of them knew my heritage. They only knew I was human, but that was enough to draw out some hatred in the end."

"Hatred seems like a harsh word, are you sure it wasn't misunderstanding?" He leaned back in the leather office chair and watched her.

"I'm sure. Even the tigress I thought was my best friend, Edith, turned against me. We grew up together, but she couldn't understand why I would care about *her kind* when I was *only* human. There was such hatred in her tone."

"I'll be sure to have a nice conversation with Edith when we find her."

"We won't, she was killed, and her final thoughts of me were that I was proposing this so it would advance shifters living alongside humans."

He raised an eyebrow at that. "Isn't that a good thing?"

"Except she thought I was doing it to eliminate the shifter species. That I wanted to construct some type of revenge against shifters because I felt left out." She pulled her legs up against her chest, hugging them to her body. "I never felt excluded because I couldn't shift. Were those feelings always there from those I considered my family and I just missed the clues?"

"Come here, angel." He slid his chair back and patted his lap.

"Sex—"

"It's not about sex, it's about comfort." He held out his hand to her and when she came, he pulled her into his lap. "It's not always about sex."

"But when it is, you make it worth it," she teased and snuggled against his chest.

"Would you want it any other way?"

"Hell no, the sex is amazing. Just maybe…more of it?" She slid her hand under his shirt, teasing along the perfect contours of his chest. Damn, this man was perfect, and she just wanted more of him—of both him and Turi. It seemed to be more than just mating desire. The need deep inside felt like pure love.

"Now that, my angel, can be arranged." He leaned forward and claimed her mouth. The spiciness from the coffee lingered on his lips, mixing with the hazelnut creamer he'd added to it.

She slid around on his lap until she was straddling his waist and slipped her tongue into his mouth. Devouring the sweetness and spiciness, she cupped the back of his head. Their tongues danced together in the heat of passion, and she wanted more. Tugging his shirt up his chest she wanted him naked and inside of her.

She broke the kiss, dragging her teeth over his bottom lip. "I need you."

"My thoughts exactly." He stood up, lifting her with him and carried her across the room to the chaise lounge where she had been before. As he gently sat her down, she pulled off his shirt and allowed him to reciprocate. "Naked, now."

In one smooth motion, she slid the black yoga pants down her legs, her gaze on him as he stripped from his jeans and boxers. Damn, was he one fine specimen of manhood. He set her blood boiling, and her core heated with desire.

"Your bra."

He stood before her. Sunlight caressed his bronzed skin, and as he moved, his powerful muscles flexed and contracted. She allowed her gaze to roam as she drank in the sight of him and felt a smile pulling at her lips as her gaze fell on his shaft, hard and ready. "Always willing, aren't you?" she purred as she unhooked her bra and allowed it to slip off. She pushed her breasts forward as she tossed her undergarment over the back of the chaise lounge. "I want to taste you." Without waiting she dropped to her knees before him, sliding her hand down his chest until she reached his shaft. Smiling, she met his startled gaze as she took him in her hand and slowly caressed his length.

"My angel." With a low growl in the back of his throat, he wrapped his arm around hers and tried to pull her back up.

"Let me." She leaned forward, kissing his tip before letting him slip between her lips. Keeping her hand at the base, she took him into her mouth, tasting the saltiness, and rolling her tongue along his head. Gently, her teeth teased as she took as much of him in her mouth as she could.

He tangled his hand in the strands of her hair, holding her close, demanding she take more. Her mouth worked up and down the length of him. She loved how he arched into her, as if he couldn't get enough of her.

"My sweet angel!" He moaned, laying a hand on her shoulder. "Not like this, I want to be inside you."

Wanting the same thing, she let him slip from her mouth, and he pulled her up, lifting her into his strong arms. Holding her against him, he moved to the wall and pressed her against it.

"What are you doing?"

"I want you right here against this wall." Keeping her pinned, he adjusted her until his shaft was directly below her opening. Slipping a hand between their bodies, he eased a finger between her thighs. "So wet."

"I need you now."

With one powerful thrust, he slid into her. Even wet, she was tight without the foreplay, making each thrust full of contact both pleasurable and painful. His teeth grazed along her neck as he worked himself deeper into her, his cries of frustration filling the room, mixing with her own moans. With each thrust, her heart sped with need and desire.

He pressed his lips over hers, claiming her cries with his mouth. Their breath became ragged as he rocked in and out, finding the perfect rhythm, bringing ecstasy within reach. "Trey." His name tore from her lips in a moan as she clenched her legs tightly around his waist and her climax exploded within her.

He continued to drive his shaft into her, until with one final slam home, his own release followed. The passion and pleasure lit his eyes until they looked like small blue fires, and a roar echoed through the space.

"That was amazing." Her hands ran up his back, feeling the tight muscles under her fingertips.

He held her against his body, his shaft still nestled deep within her as they calmed. "My sweet angel, I love you."

Where those three little words would have scared her only days before, now she knew they were true. It wasn't just the mating, it was who the brothers were and she loved them both.

"I love you too, Trey Brown."

Bearing Secrets: Alaskan Tigers

Chapter Eighteen

After receiving the phone call they had all been waiting for, Turi rushed back to his cabin to share the good news. He'd expected to find Trey and Ivy in his office, where he had left them only a short while ago, working. They were still in the office all right, but work wasn't happening. Instead he walked in to his naked brother with Ivy pressed against the wall. Their activity was complete, but they were still locked in each other's embrace. He had felt their energies, the sexual tension, but he had been trying to shield Ivy from feeling the pressure while he waited for the news.

Leaning against the wall, he cleared his throat. "I see you find ways to pass the time when I'm not around."

Ivy looked over Trey's shoulder at him. "I can put off work longer and we can find a way to waste more time." Trey set her down on her feet, but neither of them moved to gather their clothes.

"Tempting." Turi wanted to push everything off his desk and have his way with Ivy, but there was something more important they had to deal with.

"Then come to me."

"If there was time I would." He promised the raging bear within him that he'd have his way with her on that desk very soon. "I just received a call...Chad's on his way. He should be landing in twenty minutes." He leaned off the doorframe, intending to go to her, but before he could cross the space, her legs give out from under her. Trey's quick reflexes were enough to catch her just before she collapsed to the floor in a heap.

"Alive?" Her voice strained with fear.

"Turi can be an ass sometimes but if Chad was dead he'd break it to you softly." He glanced to Turi as he lifted her into his arms.

"Sit her on the chaise lounge." Turi waited until she was settled with a blanket around her shoulders, before squatting down in front of her. "Chad's fine. He was where you thought he'd be."

Turi slid his thumb across her face, wiping away the wetness. *Tears, but why?* "What's the matter, love? This should be happy news."

She shook her head and more tears slid from her eyes. "Why didn't he come and find me? Why stay holed up there?"

"Mason..." Turi started to explain but more tears fell. "My love, don't cry. He searched the area, trying to find you. When he found nothing he hoped you'd managed to get away. They were waiting for Mason to heal before they could do a full search for you."

"Mason? Is he okay?"

"He was injured, but a healer from the Alaskan Tigers tended to him." Turi took her hand in his, holding it tight. "The other guard,

I didn't catch his name, wasn't so lucky. Chad did what he could for both of them but before the team could find them, the other guard died. His beast within couldn't heal all the injuries before the infection took its toll, and eventually he just gave in."

"Chad's alive," she whispered, as if she still couldn't believe it.

"My angel." Trey waited until she looked at him. "You don't have long before he'll be here, you should at least get dressed."

She looked down as if she had forgotten and smiled. "Oh."

"Trey, go run a hot bath for her," Turi ordered, rubbing his hands over hers.

"I don't have time." She shook her head, trying to stop him, but Trey was already on his way out of the room.

"You do. It will help relax you and there's nothing you can do but wait anyway." He stood, gently pulling her up against his chest. "Come on, let me pamper you. I'll wash your back and all the sensitive spots that I know Trey made sore."

"Won't that will lead to some more…soreness?" She raised an eyebrow at him as if she knew he had other ideas than just washing her beautiful body.

"If I'm lucky." He leaned down and swooped her into his arms. "Getting you naked is all I seem to think about anymore."

"I'm already naked."

"That, my beautiful mate, is what I plan to take advantage of." With ease he carried her down the short hall to their bedroom. *Their bedroom.* He loved the sound of those two little words. He still couldn't believe how quickly things had happened. One morning he was adamant about not sharing a mate with Trey and the next night she strolled into their lives and his heart.

"Bath's ready." Trey turned off the spigot of the deep Jacuzzi bathtub. Like the shower it had plenty of room that they could have both joined her but as Trey left them, he flicked the switch to the two-sided gas fireplace that formed the wall between the tub and the bedroom. "Enjoy."

Turi set her down in the tub. The jets washed over her and got the sleeves of his shirt wet. With her settled in and her head resting against the lip of the tub, he stood. "Relax for a moment."

"Gas fireplace?" Her voice was soft, and full of pure delight as the jets eased some of the tightness he knew she had been carrying not knowing Chad's fate.

"I wanted something that could be seen from both rooms. It could add to the romance, casting the warm glow across the room and then be turned off without having to worry about dealing with it." He pulled his long-sleeved shirt from his jeans and slid it over his head. "My office and the living room have the real things as you've already seen because I spend the most of my time there. Up until now the bedroom was for sleeping so the fireplace wasn't as important. If it bothers you we can change it."

"Doesn't bother me, I was just wondering why the change in this part. Though it makes me wonder why three fireplaces?"

"Power outages are common here in Alaska. We have generators, but for heat nothing beats the fireplaces."

She nodded and glanced to him. "Will you join me?"

"I thought you'd never ask." He stripped out of the rest of his clothes, giving her a little dance as he did. After all Trey wasn't the only one who could do a striptease; Turi just preferred to do it in his human form. He pumped his hips, giving her a few view of his hardening shaft. "You like this, don't you?"

"Oh, I love it, come to me." She moved deeper into the large tub so he could join her. Her back pressed up against the far side of the tub. "Aww…this is hot."

"The tub has warming walls surrounding it to keep it heated. Trey turned them on with the fireplace." He stepped into the tub causing a ripple over the top that lapped gently against her breasts.

"What a thoughtful man."

"Don't go getting soft on me, beautiful. That brother of mine has had you to himself too much, and it's only going to get worse while he does his techie crap for the forum with you." He eased into the water and pulled her onto his lap.

"You're going to be a part of it, so there's no need to be jealous." She slid her hands up his chest so she could cup either side of his face. "You've been busy, and our time together has been shorter, but that doesn't mean I love you any less."

He nuzzled her neck, marking her with his scent. "Do you realize I've been holding off saying those three little words because I didn't want to scare you away with all you've been going through, and you just said it like it was nothing?"

"It's the truth, I love you. It scared me at first to have two mates demanding my attention and more, but now I don't think I'd want it any other way."

"I love you, Ivy, and you witnessed the fight between Trey and I about sharing a mate, but you, my sweet mate, make it all worth it."

She took her hands away from his face and let them disappear under the water. "We're wasting precious time." Her fingers wrapped around his shaft, bringing it back to its full erection with only a few strokes down the length.

"Time is too precious to waste, and I want to be buried deep within you."

"On with it, bear."

He positioned her so that her knees were on either side of his hips. His fingers eased between her legs, running along the bundle of nerves before slipping a finger inside of her to see if she was ready for him. Instantly her body responded, her back arched, and a soft moan escaped from her lips. "I love that your body is constantly on edge with yearning for us, and when you finally get it, the ecstasy in your eyes is like a thousand fireworks."

"Then don't keep me waiting."

He moved his hands to her hips and lifted her. When she hovered above him, he adjusted so his shaft stood just below her entry. With his hands on her hips, he guided her down onto him. Filling her inch by inch, nearly half in, he pushed up on her hips making her rise again before entering her completely with his manhood. His steady strokes fed their desire, and his hands on her hips guided their pace, while water crashed over their bodies making tiny waves.

He leaned into her, locking his mouth on her nipple and sucked until she moaned in pleasure. Her hips increased pace, driving the force of each pump. Breaking the kiss he watched her ride him, speeding the pace with her own need until his thrusts became deeper and faster falling into a perfect rhythm.

Her body tightened around his shaft and her nails dug into his chest. "Turi!" she cried out as they both came.

Breathless, he brushed her wet hair from her face. He wanted to see her, to see her eyes and that dreamy look she got. The aftermath of amazing sex made her glow with beauty, sending a fresh wave of desire through him.

She collapsed forward, their chests pressed together as their breathing returned to normal. With his shaft still deep inside her, he wrapped his arms around her and held her tight against him. "Mate, I love you."

Bearing Secrets: Alaskan Tigers

Chapter Nineteen

Her shoulder pressed against the window frame, Ivy watched as Kallie and Milo roughhoused in their animal forms. So carefree and full of life, while she was stuck inside listening to her brother rant and rave about her mating. When she heard they had found Chad and he was alive, she was thrilled, relief washed over her, but now that he was here she just wanted him to go away.

"Damn it, Ivy, are you listening to me?" He slammed his hand down on the coffee table in front of him. The boom of the impact startled her, reminding her of the gun blasts from the attack.

"I heard you, but what do you want me to say? Things are as they are. You know how mating works, you don't have a choice. Can't you just be happy for me?"

"No!" His voice was full of such anger she had to turn toward him. "I'd rather you dead than mated to a shifter."

"*What?*" She couldn't believe her ears. Did he really just imply he'd rather she'd died in the attack than be mated to Turi and Trey?

"I *don't* want you with a shifter." He glared at her and for the first time there was more than just anger in his eyes; she couldn't quite put her finger on it, but it seemed almost like hatred.

"No, the part about how you wish I was dead." She tried to keep the anger from boiling within her, knowing that if it became out of control her mates would ride to her rescue, even if she didn't want them to.

"It's wrong for you to be with a shifter…"

"Why, because I'm human?" She stepped away from the window and advanced toward him, her fists in balls. "I can spend my whole life surrounded by shifters, but to find two that actually love me despite my heritage or the fact I'm human and that's suddenly wrong?"

"Don't get me started on the fact you're fucking two brothers!"

"No, let's stay on one topic at a time, and you can tell me why it's so wrong for me to be with a shifter." Needing to hear his answer no matter how much it might hurt, she refused to back down.

"We're interested in knowing too." She turned to the sound of Turi's voice and found him and Trey standing in the kitchen archway.

"You!" Chad growled, coming to his feet.

"Don't even think about it, Chad," she warned, knowing her brother was about to go after her mates.

"What's going to stop me?" Now that his anger had found a new target he didn't bother to turn and look at her.

"My angel, it's okay." Trey tried to reassure her as she neared them.

"No, it's not." She stepped between them, giving her mates her back so she could keep Chad in view. His anger had control of him and she knew better than to let an angry tiger out of her sight. "Chad, if you do this I'll ask you to leave *for good*."

"You're choosing these *bears*…"

She didn't like where this was going but she nodded. "If you're forcing me to make a choice, I guess I am. You know mating won't be denied, and I love them."

"How could you love them? It's only been a few days." Chad rotated his neck, something he always did before he shifted. "This bullshit about mating, they might have to suffer with the pain of being denied their mate until it drives them insane, but you're *human*. What do you know about it? You can't feel the beast crawling within you until you feel like you're being driven insane."

"Why does it always come back to me being human? I'm not lesser for that, you know." She took a deep breath and tried to keep her rage under control. With her mates so close, their anger was mixing with hers, making it harder. "For the record, I *can* feel the mating desire. To deny them would cause me just as much pain, but why would you care? You just wanted me dead."

"Then we'll find a cure. Shifters are dangerous, bears even more so. I've protected you all these years, now you just expect me to step away and let you risk your life because of some desire."

"You know what, Chad? That's it." She tossed her hair from her face. "I'm tired of this prejudice. I've always considered you my brother, and I love you, but I'm done. This double standard is absurd. I can spend my whole life surrounded by shifters, but now that I'm mated to two devoted, wonderful bears, it's an issue."

"Damn right. There's no one to keep them in line from hurting you. Do you think your heritage won't cause issues? Then what will happen when I'm not around and Mason isn't around as Alpha to protect you? They'll kill you and find a new mate, one without the baggage."

"That's enough." Turi growled. "I've stood here and listened to you, hoping you'd work through this irrational anger and support Ivy because you're her family and she loves you, but no more. We know about her heritage, and that changes nothing. We love her and will protect her—even from someone she considers family." He wrapped his arm around her waist, drawing her snugly against his body.

"Ivy was worried sick about you and now that you're here, this is how you treat her? It's a disgrace to the word *family*." Trey stepped up to her other side and wrapped his arm around her shoulders.

"They'll hurt you. Bears are notorious for hurting the ones they're supposed love. Leave with me now, or I'll wipe myself clean of this own situation, and your blood will be on their hands."

The first of what she knew would be many tears splashed down her face. "Leave. I've heard enough. I'm staying here…I love Turi and Trey, if you can't accept that then I'll grieve for you but my choice has been made."

"Don't do this, Ivy." Chad's shoulders sank; his whole body seemed to cry out that he couldn't believe what she was saying.

"Please, just leave." With her heart already breaking, she brushed away the tears. As he turned on his heel and stormed from the house, her stomach sank, and she wondered if it would be the last time she saw him.

"My sweet angel." Trey tried to sooth her, but the tears wouldn't stop.

When the front door slammed shut, her legs gave out from under her. As if knowing she'd rather stay right where she was then be carried to the sofa, the men eased her to the floor, each keeping their arms around her as they came to the floor with her.

"What happened? Why did everyone turn on me?" She couldn't figure out in such a short time how her life went from perfect to this.

"We haven't." Trey smoothed her hair out of her face.

"First Edith, now Chad. He was the last piece of family I had left."

"You have us," Turi reassured her. "And the sleuth."

"The Alaskan Tigers, Milo, Ty, Adam—"

"Trey, I think she gets the idea." Turi told his brother, which brought halfhearted laughter from her. "I know this is hard, if there is anything we can do…"

"You're already doing it." She rested her head against Turi's chiseled chest, breathing in the spiciness of his cologne and beast. "I don't know what his issue is but I'm not going to allow that to stop me from living the life I was meant to have. He won't keep me from my mates."

"He seemed to despise the fact you were mated to bears. Any history with him and bears?"

"Not that I'm aware of. Hell, it's stupid but I didn't even know there were bear shifters. Stupid…if there are tigers why wouldn't there be others?" She shook her head.

"It's not stupid, not all animals have shifter groups. I've never seem an elephant shifter." Turi smoothed his hand down her arm.

"An elephant shifter." The very idea was hilarious. If she was a shifter, there wasn't a chance in hell she wanted to shift into an elephant. She'd much rather be something dangerous like a bear, tiger, or lion.

Suddenly she straightened against Turi's body and steered back to the issue at hand. "I suspect Chad will want to leave the island soon, if your dad doesn't kick him off first. Mason will too…I should talk to him. I need to know if he's changed against me as well. He welcomed me into his clan with open arms, took my commitment to the clan with honor, but if it's all changed I need to know."

"Are you sure, angel?" Trey looked to Turi for back up.

"I know you want to protect me, but I need to know." Touched by his concern, she laced her fingers through Trey's.

"Trey, go find Mason, bring him here. I don't want her to run into Chad again, not until he gets his shit together. I won't have it—" He stopped as she tensed in his arms. "I won't apologize for protecting you. The way he spoke to you was uncalled for."

There was nothing she could say to that. How could she blame him for something that was so ingrained in them? It wasn't just the beasts within them, but also the alpha males inside them. She rose up on her knees ready to stand. She'd get this over with and then she could spend time in her mates' arms, which was where she wanted to be.

Bearing Secrets: Alaskan Tigers

Chapter Twenty

With speed and precision, Trey moved through the grounds toward the final destination: Mason's cabin. He didn't like the fact his mate was set on finding out if Mason was against her now too, but he'd do anything she asked. If, in the end, it broke her heart further, Turi and he would be there to put it back together. To help her move on and rebuild her life…no, not rebuild, but to make it better. Now with the proposal and the forum, she'd have a new purpose in her life. No one would look down on her because she was human, or treat her the way Chad did. Not on his watch. She was his now, and Heaven have mercy on the next asshole that hurt her.

The scent of Chad drifted through the air, bringing the bear to the surface and full of anger. The beast within him wanted to go after Chad, to beat the shit out of him for hurting Ivy the way he had. Ivy had been worried sick about him, and instead of showing a care, he degraded her about mating with bears, as if she had a choice.

Unable to hold it back, Trey tipped his head back and roared. After his bear was finished letting off a little steam, he was able to relax a little. The muscles in his shoulders were still tight, and anger pulsed within him, but at least he wasn't on the verge of killing his brother-in-law.

"Trey? Or are you Turi?" A man asked as Trey neared one of the two guest cabins.

"Trey." He held his hand out to the other man, the scent of the tiger and the air of authority letting him know he'd found the right person. "You must be Mason."

"That I am." With a firm grip, he shook Trey's hand. "I believe you've already had a run-in with the Captain of my Guards, Chad."

"You could say that. He seems to have a real hatred toward bears, or maybe it's just the ones his sister mated with."

"Chad's out for a run but if you have a few minutes we could sit and I could give you a little insight to your mate's brother." Mason tipped his head to the porch.

"I don't know how that will help, but okay." Trey led the way to the porch, scanning the island to check to see if Chad was returning.

Mason took a seat in one of the rockers Theodore custom built. "Chad's been very protective of Ivy all her life. To just stop doing it because she's mated is hard, but even harder because of who she's mated to."

"You mean bears." Trey's top lip curved up on one side and he couldn't stop from growling.

"Yes, but not for the reason you think. Chad's anger stems from the fact that his mother was killed by a bear, not a shifter but an actual bear. Now all he can see is anger. I don't even think Ivy knows the full details of what happened, only that she was killed while she went on a hunting trip with a group of clan members."

"How does something like that happen? She should have sensed the bear long before he was able to get close enough to endanger her life." Trey leaned against the porch railing, watching Mason.

"It was mostly women on the trip, kind of a getaway from the mates and kids. Alcohol and drugs played a part, and she was attacked while she was unaware. The others took off leaving her behind, and she was killed."

Trey silently sat there for a moment with many things running through his head. Even after hearing what had happened to Chad's mother, it didn't give him a valid excuse to treat Ivy the way he did. "I understand, but Ivy deserved better than being the target of Chad's anger. He knows she had no control over who she mated. Wishing her dead was a dagger through the heart for her."

"I've already spoken to him about it, but all he can see is his belief that she'll end up dead like his mother." Mason ran a hand over the leg of his jeans. "Due to that, Chad and I will be leaving this afternoon. It will give him time to cool off, and hopefully he can come to his senses."

"That might be for the best." Trey nodded. Without Chad on the island, he wouldn't have to worry about Ivy getting hurt by his nasty comments. "I came to find you because Ivy would like to speak to you. She needs to know if you've turned against her as well."

"I'll speak with her." Mason rose from the chair and came to stand next to Trey, looking out on the land and water. "She's had a rough time. Some of the clan questioned her reasoning behind this proposal, and now this. It's good she's found you and your brother, she needs the love and protection."

"Trust me, she has it. We'll protect her, even from the one she thinks is family if that's what it comes to." He turned to face Mason. "If Chad can't get past this anger over who she's mated to, then I'll have to ask that he has no contact with her. She doesn't deserve to be treated like she's less than him."

"Human or not, Ivy has always been a valued member of my clan. She was never put in areas of danger. Doing administration work kept her among the trusted of the clan and overall a cherished member. She will be missed." Mason took a moment to look at Trey before nodding. "I suspect you'll encourage her to finish the proposal. It's something that could be useful to our kind and if anyone can put together a strong case for it, she can. Know there will be opposition, most likely that stems from her being a human, but in the end it will be worth it."

"We're behind her in that, and actually we've added some suggestions. One of them being a forum where shifters can be kept updated, communicate with other clans, and more. We're still working out the details but it will be kept tightly guarded and monitored to ensure no additional dangers or threats are recorded."

"It seems she's found the perfect mates." Mason smiled before tipping his head. "What do you say we go find Ivy and put some of her fears to rest?"

Trey nodded, and pushed off the railing. "She needs to know where Chad's anger comes from."

"Once we leave, you can tell her that. I only want to relieve her doubts when it comes to me and any of the Arizona Tigers who are left." Mason followed Trey down the steps. "Over the years she has become like a daughter to me, she needs to know nothing has changed. I'm happy she's found mates who don't think less of her because she's human and who can protect her from whatever the future holds."

As they made their way back to Ivy, Trey was relieved about Mason's stance. Knowing there wasn't yet more opposition against Ivy made it easier for him to allow another man close to his mate. There was no doubt in his mind that if Mason had been as full of hatred as Chad, he wouldn't allow him within a hundred yards of her. She was his mate and he'd protect her, even if she didn't want him to.

Taber stepped out of the cabin he used when on the island and waved to them. "Mason, wheels up in thirty."

"We'll be there. Thanks." Mason nodded.

"You and the others leaving?" Trey hoped that Kallie and Courtney might be around a little longer in case Ivy needed a woman to talk to after what she went through with Chad.

Taber shook his head. "I'm flying them to the Alaskan Tigers' compound, but I'll be back by dinner. Something up?"

"Just thought before you leave a family dinner would be beneficial to Ivy, especially having the women there. Maybe tomorrow?" Trey shoved his hands into the pockets of his jeans.

"Sure." Taber nodded and leaned against the porch pillar. "We could grill out, have some steaks, Mom's delicious macaroni salad, and the works."

"Tomorrow it is. I better get back to Ivy." Trey continued leading Mason the short distance to Turi's cabin, the one that had become theirs now that they'd found Ivy.

"Ivy's going to need the support of not only you and Turi but your whole family," Mason said, his brow furrowed in thought. "Having two sisters-in-law instead of just more men, might be what she needs. The only close female friend she had turned against her at the very end. Hopefully, Kallie and Courtney can help her learn to trust again."

Trey caught an expression of sadness rushing over Mason's face before he tucked it away and turned to look toward the woods.

"Don't worry about her, we'll take good care of her." He smirked, knowing the tiger had good motives, but Turi couldn't wait for him to be gone. With the last visual reminder of her past life departed, maybe she could embrace her new life and the possibilities it held.

Chapter Twenty-One

Snuggled on the sofa with a blanket around her shoulders and a mug of tea Trey had so thoughtfully brought her, Ivy let the stress of the day roll away from her. Mason's visit had left her full of conflicting emotions but also gave her peace knowing he hadn't turned against her too. The thought of her former Alpha without his clan pained her almost as much as the loss of them. For the first time in her life, she felt like an orphan. No one was left now that Chad had turned on her. No one except her mates, and Mason.

She was her own woman, one who'd always been strong, but now her real strength was emerging. Tomorrow the sun would come up and she'd embrace a new life, with new goals and desires. She'd dive back into the proposal and make it better than ever. Maybe in time Chad would come around, but even then she knew things would never be the same between them. There would always be the tension and painful memories of his anger toward her and her mates. That concern was for another day. Tonight she would seek comfort in the arms of her men.

"Anything I can get you?" Turi asked, coming back from the kitchen where the twins had been starting dinner.

"You." She held out her hand to him. "Will you join me?"

"I'd do anything for you." He crossed the room in three quick strides, and sank down next to her on the sofa. "I'm sorry for everything…"

Setting her mug aside, she snuggled into his chest, wrapping her arm around his waist and holding him close. The spicy aroma of cologne and his beast teased along her senses, making her want to press her face against him. "None of it's your fault."

"That might be the case, but when one mate is hurting we all feel it." He wrapped his arm around her, his finger playing gently down her arm. "I know you're still hurting after Chad's words, but maybe he'll come around. He just needs time to adjust to this."

"My brother has never come around for anything. It's always been his way or no way, but I can't think about that now. Instead, I need to focus on us. This is a time for us to grow as a trio, to move forward, and for me to start a new life. Having you, Trey, and your family, I couldn't ask for more."

Trey popped his head around the corner and glanced at them. "I heard my name."

"Come join us." She slipped her legs off the sofa so that he could come and sit on the other side of her. "I want you both."

He came to her, the jeans riding low on his hips, with the tight T-shirt just barely meeting them. "What did you have in mind, my angel?"

"Wicked things." When he sat down next to her, she looped her leg over his.

"A woman after my own heart," he teased, pressing his body along hers.

"Tonight I want to forget everything and just enjoy us. Right now, this mating is what matters. The proposal, the forum, and everything else can wait until tomorrow. Tonight, make me forget all that's wrong in the world."

"That, my angel, we can do." Trey turned enough to plant soft kisses along her shoulder and up toward her ear.

With a soft moan, she arched her neck into his caresses. "Not yet. I want to change first. When I get back, you'd better be ready." She slipped from between them, giving them a saucy look before she moved down the hall toward their bedroom.

Once out of their sight, she jogged to the bedroom, unzipping the suitcase she had yet to unpack, and lifted the package from Kallie. The handwritten note attached caught her attention again.

This will stop those twins in their tracks.

Inside the thick brown paper was a creamy white baby-doll nighty with light blue trim. Never seeing a reason for anything sexy before, she felt a rush of excitement course through her. She stripped her clothes off quickly and pulled the nighty over her head.

A glance in the mirror, a fluff of her blonde hair, and she was ready. She took a deep breath and made her way back to the men waiting for her. They'd make her forget her troubles.

"My angel, we're ready for you," Trey called.

"I'm coming." She sped up her pace. "You better be naked and ready."

"Oh, we are," they replied just as she came around the corner.

Ivy skidded to a stop. Her lungs squeezed against her heart as she took in the sight before her. A bed of blankets and makeshift pillows had been laid out before the fireplace, with candles adding to the glow from the roaring fire.

"It's beautiful." When they didn't reply or even move toward her she met their gaze. "What?"

"Damn, woman. You're beautiful."

"My sweet angel, you're gorgeous." Trey echoed Turi's sentiments in his own words.

"You like it, then?" She teased as if she'd been worried about it.

"Yes would be an understatement." Trey nodded, his shaft standing at attention.

"I love it, but want you naked. I want to see the fire dancing off your body as your face tightens and your body convulses around my dick." Turi advanced to her, his fingers grabbing the hem of the nighty and sliding it up past her hips.

Trey knelt on the makeshift bed and held a hand out to her. "Come here."

Before she could do as he asked Turi pulled the baby-doll over her head, making her as naked as they were. "Lie down near the fire so you don't get chilled, and let us show you how amazingly sexy we find you."

Lying in the middle of the makeshift bed, all her worries disappeared, need and desire replacing them. "Please…" She reached out, her hand landing firmly on Turi's chest, who was kneeling between her legs, his erection pressed tight against her thigh. Trey laid beside her, his lips claiming her nipple. They had her captive between their bodies, making her feel safe and wanted.

Turi's fingers slipped between her legs and teased her pussy, dragging pleasure from her in hard, hot waves. His fingers thrust into her as his thumb continued to wring more pleasure from her core. He quickly eased down her body, replacing his fingers with his mouth. His tongue did all the work, flicking gently across her mound until she was wiggling beneath him, her climax nearing.

Trey moved up her body, claiming her mouth; her moans died on her lips as he thrust his tongue deep inside. Their tongues danced, mixing the spiciness of his coffee with the sweetness of her tea. He pulled back enough to graze his teeth over her lower lip and let her cries of frustration escape.

"I need one of you inside me. Please…"

Without hesitation, Turi gave one last kiss to her most sensitive area and pulled back. He angled himself between her legs, his fingers digging into her thighs as he shoved his shaft into her. There was no teasing, no easing in slowly. Instead, he slammed his length into her in one hard pump. Her body took him in, throbbing against his erection as darts of pleasure spiraled outward from their connection. Breathing became difficult as he retreated only to thrust into her again, harder this time. As he picked up the rhythm, he drove into her again and again, rigid and powerful, sending the outside world far away from her thoughts. This wasn't the loving of a man; it was the claiming by a mate.

Trey scooted up until he could kneel before her, his hard length jutting toward her. Without invitation, she took him into her mouth, working her way to the base. She used her hand to work the end of the hard shaft, moving her mouth up and down the length, slowly at the tip.

With a deep groan he cupped the back of her head and sped her pace. Forcing her to take him harder and faster, until she was trapped in the tempo of their motions. Working together, they drove intense pleasure from her body. Rocking together in perfect harmony, ecstasy began to overwhelm her. Her moans echoed around Trey's shaft as he pumped faster, his own climax near detonation. Digging her nails into the back of Trey's thighs, she held on to him as every pump sent pulses exploding through her. She came apart at the seams, her inner muscles clenching around Turi as he continued to drive his shaft into her.

Turi slammed home one last time before his orgasm filled her and he tipped his head back and roared. Trey hadn't finished yet. He slammed into her mouth, forcing her to take all of him. Soft grunts escaped him as he worked to find his own release. He pushed deep within her mouth one final time, forcing her to swallow his juices, as another wild climax spiraled through her.

Trey slipped from her lips and leaned against the sofa, his eyes closed. Still reeling, she tugged his hand until he scooted down to lay next to her.

Eventually, her breathing returned to normal, and she cuddled against both of her mates, contented. She let the thoughts of having them by her sides always play through her mind. It was different from what she had expected, but it was just what she needed and never knew she wanted.

Bearing Secrets: Alaskan Tigers

Chapter Twenty-Two

The last few weeks had gone by without a hitch, and Ivy was settling into the Brown family with her mates. Their work on the proposal and forum was making huge strides. Soon it would be complete and they could launch the forum. The proposal would land on Ty and Tabitha's laps, and they'd be able to look it over and make a decision on how to proceed.

For the first time in her life, everything was falling into place. The only thing missing was the contact from Chad. There was no call or even a text from him. The only difference from when she arrived was she no longer had to worry what happened to him. He was alive, living his life; he just didn't want anything to do with her.

"Anyone home?" Ava called as she opened the sliding glass door and entered.

"In here," Ivy answered, glancing up from the book that hadn't really been holding her interest.

Ava appeared through the archway wearing a warm smile.

"The boys are out fishing," Ivy told her. "They've demanded freshly caught salmon for dinner tonight."

"Sounds like my sons." Ava raised the cake platter in her hands. "I come bearing gifts, chocolate mousse cake with a chocolate chip coating around the sides, and shredded pieces of white chocolate on the top."

"Sounds delicious."

"It's so delicious it melts on your tongue. Make sure you get some before the boys tear into it, or it will be gone before you can bat an eyelash."

"Why don't you join me and we'll do that now?" Ivy set her book aside and stood.

"I'd be honored. You grab drinks and I'll cut." Ava took the cake to the counter, while Ivy grabbed two mugs and poured the coffee she knew her mother-in-law favored. "It's nice to have another woman on the island."

"You have Bev too."

"Bev and I can only stand each other for short bouts. Put us in a room together for more than an hour and we're at each other's throats." She brought the plates to the table and sat. "You, on the other hand…I couldn't have asked for a better woman for my boys. Turi and Trey have changed since you've come into their life."

"What do you mean?" Ivy took a bite of the cake, letting the smoothness glide over her tongue. "Oh, this is heavenly."

"Told you." Ava smirked, her tone a little cocky, and deservedly so. If there was one thing she could do beyond anyone else, it was bake. "Trey's been taking more of an interest in the sleuth responsibilities, working alongside Turi, not against him. Even taking over some of the duties himself, handling problems that might arise without finding someone else. The forum is finally being started and they're working together on it. There's a closeness to the twins I haven't seen since they were cubs." She captured Ivy's gaze and smiled, her eyes a little misty. "It's all because of you."

"I can't take all of the credit."

"Child, it's your doing." Ava took another bite of the cake before setting her fork aside. "Those boys are finally working together as a team instead of fighting each other at every move."

Ivy sat there silently, unsure what to say to that. She had noticed changes in her men since she'd arrived. Each having their own personalities but still finding a way to mesh together allowing them to be the ultimate trio.

They had nearly finished the slices of cake when Ava looked up at her. "Do you mind if I'm honest with you?"

"No." She shook her head, her heart beating a little faster, wondering what Ava thought she needed the extra caution for.

"Growing up with two fathers, I saw how they loved and cherished my mother, and when I came of age to find a mate I sought out that same thing. I didn't want one mate, I wanted two to treasure me."

"I was always told shifters don't have a choice in their mates."

Ava shook her head. "They don't, but that didn't stop me from trying to fight it. When Devon touched me, his bear roared to life and the mating connection began, I fought it like someone fights an untimely death. I didn't want it. Devon was a great guy, but he wasn't the one I wanted. Somewhere out there I believed there were mates searching for me as I searched for them. I had to be destined to have the same relationship as my mother; after all, I witnessed firsthand the beauty of it."

"I see the love you and Devon share," Ivy reasoned, because what she witnessed couldn't be a facade.

"After I learned to accept I wouldn't get what I wanted…actually that wasn't until after the torture of denying a mate set in…then I was able to learn to love him. Devon is a wonderful man, an amazing mate, and a great father. Now I wouldn't change who I ended up with, but back then there was some anger and hostility because I felt like he denied me the same happiness my mother had." She stared off into space, sadness etched into her features as if she was remembering the pain of those days.

"Why are you telling me this?" Ivy cupped her coffee mug and watched the older woman over the rim.

"I want you to understand how lucky you are. That there are going to be trials and tribulations, but in the end you have two wonderful mates by your side. I'm not just saying that because they're my sons and I raised them, but because I know they will protect and love you." Ava reached across the table and laid her hand over Ivy's. "The boys can see you're hurting now because of Chad, and they want to make it right."

"There's nothing they can do. My brother is a stubborn pain in the ass. He won't come around until he's ready…if he's ever ready."

Her gaze drifted away and out the window to the creek where her men were frolicking in bear form.

"It doesn't stop them from trying. If I know my boys, they'll be overbearing, I just want you to remember they're trying to take your pain away, not add to it. They might go about it the wrong way and I'm sure there will be times they'll drive you crazy, but they love you."

Ivy watched the twins splashing around just off the beach. "I was just the opposite. I searched for a mate, never sure I would find one since I wasn't a shifter, but I wanted what I saw others had. I never realized some shifters mated with more than one, or that I'd even want that."

"Now?" Ava prodded.

Her lips curled up in a smile, and a freedom paused through her. "Now I couldn't picture my life without those two. Sure the snoring and growling in their sleep gets a bit much, especially when it's in surround sound." She laughed at her own joke, as she thought about how safe it felt snuggled between them in bed, even if she had to listen to all their noise.

"Image that with a house full of male bears," Ava joked.

"Thanks, now I have something to look forward to when children come along." Ivy laughed, sending a rush of infectious giggles through both of them.

"Children?" Ava tried to gain control of her giggles, but was failing miserably. "Will you be making me a grandmother soon?"

"I don't know about soon, but I've always wanted children."

Ava shot up from her chair and rushed around the table. "I'm so happy." She pulled her out of the chair and wrapped her arms tight around Ivy. "Taber and Thorben tell me Kallie needs more time to adjust before children are brought into it. After years of captivity, there are things she's making up for. I started applying pressure to Tad while they were here, but he told me he and Milo agreed it would happen when it happened. What kind of logic is that?"

"I take it you want lots of little grandbabies," Ivy joked as if Ava's excitement wasn't enough of a clue.

"Oh yes, lots of little cubs—babies. Oh, hell I don't care what they are. Bears, tigers, humans, they could be monkeys for all I care. I just want lots of them, so I can spoil them rotten."

"I think your sons would have an issue if I birthed monkeys," she teased.

Talking about children sent an exciting warmth through her. She was blissfully happy with her life, her mates, and the idea of starting a family. The future for shifters had already proven it was going to be a dangerous one, so she see could see no reason to wait. The excitement of having children bloomed through her, and she smiled. She'd be sure to speak with her men about the possibilities.

Chapter Twenty-Three

After an afternoon of frolicking in the water, Trey felt better than he had in months. There was ease between him and Turi they'd never had before, one that allowed them to spend a day screwing around and fishing together. Now with a basket of freshly caught salmon, they made their way back inside.

"You two better dry off before you step one foot into this house." Ivy threw towels at them as he opened the door.

"Damn, she sounds just like Mom," Turi bitched before setting the basket aside and grabbing one of the towels from Trey.

"Don't give me that tone or I'll make sure you end up with blue balls until you're so horny you're humping trees." She stood there with her hands on her hips watching them as they dried off.

"Are you enjoying the show, my sweet angel? Does the water dripping off our naked bodies get you wet?" Trey shook his hips, sending his erection bouncing.

"Oh, yes…but first of all, Turi got a call from Taber." As Turi leaned in giving her a quick kiss on the cheek before moving past her to return the call, she looked at Trey. "You need to clean those fish if you think I'm cooking them."

"What about having it raw?" Now dry, he tossed the towel over his shoulder and picked up the basket.

"I'm not a bear and unless we're doing sushi, it isn't happening. I'll make some for dinner and since you caught enough for an army, once it's clean you can put it in the smoker. Smoked salmon is delicious with cream cheese, red onions, and capers or even a bagel."

"Okay, angel. Let me grab my jeans and I'll clean these." He set the basket back down, leaving it outside since he figured she'd prefer he clean the fish at the outside station instead of in the kitchen. "Then tonight I'll show you just what this naked body can do."

"I'll hold you to that." She wiggled her eyebrows and let her hand slide along the curve of his hip until she could tease the hairs at the base of his groin.

"I saw Mom here a bit ago." He hoped she'd get that he was asking about the visit.

"She brought a cake, of which you may have a slice *after* dinner. We were talking about you two, children, mating, and life. I love your mother."

"As she does, but I hope she isn't pressuring you into giving her grandchildren."

"Why? Is it so wrong to want children? Don't you want any?"

The questions flew at him one after another. "Yes, I want a few little ones of my own, but there's no rush."

"Why not? This world we live in isn't getting any better. Why not live life to the fullest and do everything we've wanted, including having children?"

He wrapped his arms around her. "There's no reason I can think of. If you're ready for children, then we can work on that tonight."

"Soon. Tonight I have other plans."

"That sounds naughty, and I like it." He lowered his head and claimed her lips; the lingering chocolate had him slipping his tongue into her mouth. When he pulled away, she was breathless. "You taste delicious."

"You only want me for the sweets your mother keeps using as an excuse to visit," she teased, her hands reaching around him to cup his butt cheeks. "Now get those fish cleaned, I want some smoked salmon, and then you and Turi naked."

"I'm already naked."

"*Tonight.*" She shook her head.

"So demanding, mate." With one last kiss, he let her go and went in search of a pair of jeans.

He padded through to what used to be Turi's master bedroom, but had now become theirs. It was amazing how quickly things had changed. In a matter of weeks, he had fallen in love with Ivy, and couldn't picture his life without her by his side. How had he managed before?

* * *

It was funny how one little call could change everything in someone's life. Knowing the news he had to deliver wouldn't make his mate happy, Turi slipped out the back door and headed for Trey where he was cleaning fish. When he broke the news, Ivy was going to need them both at her side.

"If you've come to help, your timing is shitty. I'm just cleaning up. The fish for dinner is there and the rest is in the smoker." Trey nodded to the bowl.

"No, I've come to get you. We need to tell Ivy about her brother." Turi leaned against the counter, his gaze on the house.

"What do you mean?"

"Chad left a letter for her, and took off. Ty sent a team in search of him but there's no trace. He's vanished."

"You don't think he'll come back here, do you?" Trey dried his hands on a towel and then tossed it on the table.

"I don't think he's that stupid, but we need to be on guard. Chad's angry enough that he could believe what he said about thinking it better if she was dead rather than with us. He could come after her if he lets his tiger control him."

"We won't let harm come to her." Trey's fists clenched. "I should have taught him a lesson when he was here for how he treated her."

"There's nothing we can do about that now. We need to focus on Ivy. After all she's been through, this is another blow, and that might be too much for her to handle now."

"Naw." Trey shook his head. "Our mate is too tough to let this defeat her. She's a strong woman and with us by her side she can't lose. Which reminds me, did she mention to you that she wants to try for a family?"

"What?" Turi tore his gaze away from the house and looked at his twin.

"Mom got to her while we were fishing and somehow that led to her wanting to have a family. Not tonight, though." He grinned. "She said she has naughty plans in mind for tonight. But soon."

"Well, that should please Mom." The idea of having children both excited and terrified Turi, but he didn't let it show. "She's wanted grandchildren since before any of us mated."

"I'm sure Mom will be thrilled when one of our mates is pregnant." Trey grabbed the cleaned fish. "Tonight we've got let her know about Chad. Let's go get this over with."

With a deep sense of dread, Turi followed his brother, who was already heading back to the house. Nothing was going to make this easier, especially not delaying. It was best to get it over with and then be there to comfort her, a shoulder to cry on, someone to vent to. Whatever way she needed them, they'd be there, holding her hand and making sure she got through it intact. Mating was about more than just sex and continuing their species, it was also about being there for each other, loving each other even through the hardest times. That was what he planned to do for Ivy.

Bearing Secrets: Alaskan Tigers

Chapter Twenty-Four

Staring out the window, watching the waves crash onto the beach as the sun sank low, casting warm red and pink streaks through the sky, Ivy tried to move past her anger. She was tired of Chad's attitude. She understood that having his mother killed by a bear had left its scars but there was a big difference between bears and bear shifters. The biggest of them being logical thought. When shifters changed form, they still held their willpower and thoughts as they would in human form. They wouldn't kill an innocent person. Even being a shifter and knowing there was a difference, Chad couldn't separate the two. All he saw when he looked at the Browns was the same animal that killed his mother.

She had tried to be understanding, to let him have his fit and leave the island without a goodbye. She even tried to forget he had wished her dead. But no longer could she put it all aside. Chad was acting like an ass, and she'd had enough. Taking off with only a note for Mason to find, he hadn't just abandoned them. Leaving her behind when she wanted him to share in her happiness, he had left behind the position he worked so hard for, and put Mason in more danger. As the only Elder guard left to protect Mason, it was a serious lapse in judgment that she couldn't overlook, not when Mason had opened his clan to her.

A ball of animosity and disappointment rolled around her stomach, growing bigger with each passing second. Even though it was Chad who had disappointed, she was the one left to deal with the outcome. Though she might never return to the Arizona Tigers, even after Mason had ensured her she'd always be welcome, the guilt of Chad's actions weighed on her shoulders. There had to be something she could do to help Mason, to make sure he was safe even though he had no guards protecting him.

"Ivy…" Turi's boots echoed on the hardwood floors as he neared.

Not wanting him to see the tears, she quickly she reached up and brushed them away. "I'm fine."

"You can't lie to a mate." He slipped his arm around her waist and tugged her against his massive chest.

She let him because she wanted the comfort he could give. To feel his arms around her, her head pressed against his toned chest made it almost worth her heartache. She laid her hand over his heart, feeling the beat under her fingertips, and knew this was what mattered.

My mates.

There was nothing she could do to protect Mason, to defeat Randolph or the rogues. What she *could* do was love her men with everything she had. She could monitor the forum, follow virtual leads, and that would have to be enough.

They stood there, locked together, until long after the sun had finished its descent, before she finally looked up at him. "What's going to happen to Mason now? With no Elder guards or clan, he's like a lone tiger. He's too strong to submit to another Alpha."

"It will be his choice, but he could rebuild his land and clan. With Tabitha taking control as Queen of the Tigers, there are others out there who need a clan that will follow her. They'd leave their own clans that are against her and come. Others who are in clans that support her might come for the promotions. He'll need new guards and if anyone can help him find suitable guards it will be Ty." He rubbed small circles down her back. "If he wants to rebuild, he'll find a way."

"He said I'd always been a part of the Arizona Tigers, even though I mated with you and Trey and would make my home here. But now things have changed."

"I don't think they have. The clan might be different but there will always be a place for you there. Mason will make sure of it. You said it yourself…he was like a father figure to you. Do you really think he'd just cast you out?"

"Chad did, and we were raised as siblings."

"Chad's an asshole," Trey announced as he came up behind them.

"Nice way to talk about your brother-in-law." She reached toward him, wanting to feel his hard strength against her too.

"I'm sorry, my angel." He pressed his body against her back. "Sometimes I don't know when to hold my tongue."

"It's okay, Trey. I don't want to admit it but he's an ass." She pressed her body into his and let her head fall back against his chest, while still holding on to Turi. "No one has any idea where he went, or if he'll ever come back. He tore me to pieces, and even after all he's done, I still love him."

"Why wouldn't you? He's family and that bond is thicker than water." Turi kissed the top of her forehead.

"Only for humans."

"Why do you say that?" Trey nuzzled her neck, planting light kisses there.

"It was drilled into me all my life. I was human and had bonds to those around me that they didn't share. Chad's mother raised me, but I was never allowed to call her by anything but her name. She was actually my aunt, but I couldn't even call her that. She was a kind woman for taking me in but my childhood wasn't anything like you see on television or read in books. There was no one to tuck me into bed and read me a bedtime story. Chad and I were close because we're close in age, less than a year separates us."

"But you said before the clan accepted you, at least you thought until you started working on your proposal. That's when Edith and you had the disagreement, right before the attack." Turi frowned.

"They did. I know it sounds like I'm contradicting myself. They accepted me, but when I would push for more than they could give, they'd remind me where my place was. I was still very young when

I stopped pushing for more, and things smoothed out, but I still remember wanting the bond with them I felt inside of me. I don't know if that makes sense, maybe I'm not explaining it right."

"Shhh, love." Turi tightened his grip on her arm. "Tigers are devoted only to their mate and children. When their children are old enough they normally venture to other clans to make a name for themselves. Parents often have little to do with them after they reach eighteen. That is not the case with all shifters."

"I see your family is different." The fact that the Browns were different thrilled her; finally she had the family she longed for, even a motherly figure in Ava.

"Even among the bears our sleuth is unusual," Trey admitted. "Most live on their own, only coming together for events. Whereas our family enjoys being close. Mom absolutely hates the fact that three of her sons are gone."

"While they were here, she clung to them like they've been gone for years," Turi added. "It had only been a couple months since they were here, even less for Tad since he just mated with Courtney and Milo."

"Your mom has such a big heart, and she welcomed me into the fold quickly. It's nice that she comes over to visit almost every day, I just wish she didn't feel like she had to bring something as an excuse."

"No excuse there, my angel. Mom is always baking or cooking. She's always brought food to us when we didn't join her for dinner, and there're always sweets in the houses." Trey nibbled her neck. "None as sweet as you, though."

"My bears and your sweets." She arched her neck giving Trey a better angle.

"How about we take our mate to bed and ease away the worries that have these muscles so tight?" Turi suggested before bending his knees and picking her up.

"What about my smoked salmon you promised?" She looked over Turi's shoulder to Trey who was following behind them.

"I'll bring you some after we have our wicked way with you." Making his way down the hall, Trey was already stripping off his clothes. "It will be a good snack once we've turned your body into a wet noodle, and you're so sore you can barely move."

She knew they'd make good on that promise. They had done it every chance they'd gotten since they had claimed her and with each time, the mating bond grew stronger. This time, she wanted it to be different. She wanted to take control of their lovemaking, to ride them until they filled her with their juices.

Chapter Twenty-Five

Fingers flying over the keyboard, Trey glanced at the door to make sure Ivy hadn't come back from her coffee run yet. This email to Ty would hopefully put her mind at rest and give them more information on what Mason was planning. He'd keep it quiet until he knew something, which was why he wanted to contact him before she returned. He also wanted to offer his help if Mason needed anything. His mate cared for Mason, and Trey would do what he could to see that no one else she cared for was hurt. She had been through too much already and if he could spare her any pain, he'd do it.

"Not only did I bring you fresh coffee, but being the amazing woman I am, I brought you a bear claw."

Just as he hit send, she set the coffee and plate to the side of his laptop.

"No wonder I picked you as a mate," he teased, grabbing the bear claw.

"You didn't have a choice. It was me who picked you and Turi." She joined in on his joke, trying to take credit for the perfect match. "Speaking of which, where is my workaholic mate?"

"He and Theodore are out cutting down trees for firewood and lumber for Theodore's furniture."

"Furniture?"

"Theodore has made almost every piece of furniture in the cabins. He's great with his hands and does amazing details. He also does custom work to sell. Right now he's working on a new bed for Tad. With three mates you need a large bed, especially when one's a bear. A king size bed just won't do, so we make our own." He explained in between bites of his treat.

"So that's why ours is so big. The other night when the snoring woke me…" She gave him a look that could shoot daggers before continuing. "I noticed the details along the headboard. It's amazing work."

"All of us can do construction, we've built all the houses on the island, but Theodore is the most talented when it comes to things like that."

"That's an idea." She propped her hip onto the corner of the desk. "We should add a board on the forum with things like this. It could get the word out for Theodore's amazing work, and I'm sure it would help other creative artisans. Like a classified section."

"I'll add it to the list." He wiped his fingers off on his jeans and grabbed the pen to write.

"I brought you a napkin." She nodded to the white napkin next to the empty plate.

"You're turning more like Mom every day, and I'm not sure that's a good thing." He took a sip of the coffee to wash down the bear claw. "My sweet angel, bears are messy."

"I'm going to house train you both," she teased. "Now how's the forum coming along?"

He turned the laptop enough that she could see the basic design. "I have to add the different categories you want, as well as the different levels of activities for the followers, but we should be ready to launch in, say, two weeks. That will give me time to get the Alpha side done as well."

"That side will be separate, right?"

"Yes. Only approved Alphas will have access to all of it. There will be a separate part that will be open to the Captain of the Alphas guards, since some of the information shared there will be beneficial in them keeping their Alpha safe. The private part within the Alpha section will be only for the Alphas and Lieutenants of approved clans. It will not be open to anyone who has not vowed their loyalties to Tabitha."

"Will that be the same with the members' area?"

"Yes, we need to safeguard it. Each possible member will need to be checked out to ensure there is no harassment, to make sure we're not putting anyone in danger. With most, all we'll have to do is check the Alpha, see if they're committed to Tabitha, then everything is fine. If someone is applying that isn't a member of a devoted clan, we'll need to do additional checks." He clicked a few buttons to show her the pages where they'd apply to be a member. "They'll fill out the information here, and with the three of us, it shouldn't take long to approve them. If we need more help we'll get the rest of the family."

"This is amazing." Her eyes traveled from left to right as she read the screen. "What about something with the type of shifter?"

"Right now it will only be open to tigers, my family, and Leo. So we don't need it yet, but I'll add it later."

"Leo?"

"Sheriff Leo Lutz of Nome, he's a lion shifter in hiding." He laid his hand over hers. "No one but Dad, my brothers, and Milo know."

"Dang, it could have worked in my proposal, but I won't say anything." She tucked a strand of her hair behind her ear. "It's nice to have someone who knows the secret working *for* you, not against."

"Yes, it can be." He nodded. "Now if you want this finished, I need to get back to work."

"You're turning into a workaholic like your brother." She leaned across the desk and lightly kissed his lips. "I want to finish the proposal anyway. I want Ty and Tabitha to have it before the forum goes live."

She slipped off the desk, going back to her spot by the window and her proposal, while all he wanted to do was go to her. He pictured spreading her over the back of the sofa and burying himself deep within her until she screamed his name.

The ding of his email pulled his thoughts away. With one last glance at Ivy, he slid his laptop back in front of him and clicked the email icon. A rush of excitement sent his mouse across the screen to open the message from Ty. Quickly reading it, he knew that it would help relieve some of the stress on Ivy's shoulders.

"Mate." He waited until she looked up. "I contacted Ty and he just got back to me. Mason is selecting guards and will rebuild. There's a lead on two members who might have survived, and a team is searching."

"Oh, that's wonderful." The smile she had when he first told her the news quickly diminished.

"You're still feeling bad about Chad." He bit his tongue to keep from saying that she had no reason to feel upset about it.

"I'm glad Mason won't let this ruin him. He's a good Alpha, well…not that I know any other Alphas. He keeps control while still being understanding."

"I haven't had contact with him until he came to the island, but I know he's been committed to Tabitha since she took her place as Queen. That's what matters to me. It will mean one less clan we will have to fight against, and more tigers on our side." He leaned back in the chair. "Mason will gather guards and stay at the Alaskan Tigers compound for now, while he has a team rebuilding the land in Arizona."

"At least he will be safe even though Chad abandoned his duties."

"Well he's found a new Captain of his Guards. Carran, he's a black tiger and has been part of Tabitha's guard for some time now." Trey hoped that the knowledge of someone else protecting Mason would help ease any remaining worry.

"A black tiger? I thought they were a thing of legends." She set her laptop aside and leaned forward, her elbows on her knees. "Wait, Carran? He's the one who rescued me in Arizona. He lowered himself into the debris to get me out."

"I own him my life then." He took a long drink of his coffee. "He's the only one known to be living. Does the fact that someone is guarding him make you feel better?"

"Actually it does."

"Good, now back to work because if you want that finished today you better get to it. Tonight we're taking off, no work." He took his own advice and closed his email to focus on the forum. He'd get done what he could before Turi returned, and then they'd have time with their mate.

He ran a hand through his hair and silently cursed. Since Ivy had come into his life, he was always thinking of ways to get her naked and new places to make love to her. He couldn't get her off his mind. The need to touch her was always there. He had become like a horny teenager again.

Epilogue

After living in Arizona, Ivy had never pictured being somewhere with a beach right outside her door, let alone freezing cold weather. Even with the chill, she strolled along the edge of the water, tossing pebbles into the crashing waves that sent white foam in the air. Day or night, Brown Island was beautiful. If it wasn't for the waves, the beautiful sunsets and rises, it was the aurora borealis putting on a fantastic light show. If she ever had to leave the island, she knew she'd never be able to find a place more stunning.

Even after being there for over two months, she hadn't grown tired of what the land had to offer. Once the weather was nicer, she had plans to explore more of it, hopefully with the company of her men if they could tear themselves away from their work long enough. The forum had begun taking more and more time for both of them, but especially Trey, leaving Turi to handle the things that came up with the sleuth.

Despite the time she had with her men was limited, it was all worth it. That forum was bringing everyone together as a whole, making things a little easier for Tabitha. It had even expanded

Theodore's business. He had more orders than he could handle, and he'd hired his cousin John to assist with some of the crafting, while he would continue to do the finer details.

To say everything was going smoothly would be an understatement. Her life was perfect. The only thing missing was Chad to celebrate in her joy. No matter where he was or what he was doing, she hoped he was happy. The thought of never seeing him again still pained her but with each day she began to accept it. Her mates made sure she didn't wallow in her sadness or worries. They'd take time out of whatever they were doing when she'd start to feel sorry for herself or the situation and show her just what she meant to them.

"Ivy." Turi jogged down the beach toward her. "I'm glad I found you."

"What's wrong?"

Turi slid to a halt in front of her, sending sand flying through the air. "I thought you'd like to know we've received our first outcry for help through the forum. A tigress from Washington D.C. sent a message just under an hour ago. She's on the run from her Alpha who found out she's supportive of Tabitha."

"Why is she running? Why not just leave the clan?"

Turi slid his hands along her arms. "The Alpha has determined that anyone found supporting Tabitha will die. She has a bounty on her head, so for her it's run or be killed."

"Wow." She took a deep breath, trying to calm the thoughts that were running through her mind. "We must help her."

"Theodore will be leaving within the hour to pick up Styx from the Alaskan Tigers. They'll check out the coordinates the woman gave and we'll go from there."

"Wait, shouldn't we go?"

"No, we have other things we need to attend to. Theodore was going to West Virginia anyway to drop off the furniture Jinx and Summer ordered. So he can fly and Styx will be the muscle. There's nothing to worry about and if things get out of control, Jinx and his clan are close by." He leaned in and kissed her cheek. "I came out here to tell you this forum is doing great. We've seen some interaction from different clans with it, but this is the first lead we've received through it."

"Maybe we could use it to locate Randolph and his gang of rogues," she suggested, still eager to have them eliminated after what they did to her clan. If Randolph was eliminated, her heritage and relation to him would no longer matter.

"Connor, the wolf shifter of the Alaskan Tigers, heads up the Nerd Crew, and his team is working on leads. Anything the forum would produce would go to him. Ty would send a team to find him." He pulled her tight against him. "Don't worry, we'll catch him."

"I don't doubt that, I only wonder how many more will die before we do. The man I heard talking on the phone after the attack said there would be more…"

"But there haven't been," Turi reassured her.

"Not yet, but he said they'd wait until our guard was down." The thought that another clan would go through what she had made her sick.

"Everyone who is devoted to Tabitha is on guard. We're as protected as we can be. Hopefully we can find them before they hurt anyone else." He ran his hands down her back, drawing small circles in the arch of her back where she kept her tension bottled. "You're safe here on the island, and you know we'd protect you."

"I know but there are so many others who don't have mates like you and Trey to protect them. Alphas have guards, but the women and children of the clans are left vulnerable."

"We can only do so much. We have suggested that the clan install fences and employ ground guards for the extra protection, though nothing is foolproof. Even the Alaskan Tigers' compound had attacks, and they have one of the best security teams around." He laid a light kiss on the top of her head. "It's a dangerous time we live in and fear is an everyday thing, but we can't let it control us or stop us from living the life we were meant to have."

Knowing he was right, she rested her head against his chest. Things were dangerous for the shifters and there was no end in sight. With the proposal on how to integrate themselves into the human world in Ty and Tabitha's hands, she'd finally realized what kind of battle they were up against. Was it one that would be worth it in the end, or would the price be more blood than they cared to spill? Only time would reveal the answer to that.

The cost made no difference if they were going to make a better life for future generations; there were battles that had to be fought. The rogues being the first. She wouldn't be on the front lines against Randolph or the rogues, but she'd do what she could to see them defeated.

One thing she knew. The battle was coming, and she'd make damn sure they were prepared. War had casualties but she wasn't about to lose anyone else she loved, not if she could stop it. She'd make sure anyone who came up against her and her mates wouldn't walk away without a fight.

The battle was only beginning.

Bearing Secrets: Alaskan Tigers

Ace in the Hole Preview

SEALed for You: Book One

Ace Diamond left behind the woman he loved when he joined the Navy SEALs. For years he focused on his career, risking life and limb on missions for his country. Now home on leave, he must face his past and ask himself if leaving her was a mistake.

At seventeen, Gwyneth London gave her heart away only to have it broken. More than a dozen years later, she decides to embrace her single life and have a child on her own. Ready to start over in her hometown, she doesn't expect to see the man who still holds her heart, but when he walks back into her life she's unable to push him away.

Can Gwyneth and Ace claim the life they were supposed to have, or will they let love pass them by?

Bearing Secrets: Alaskan Tigers

Chapter One

Ace Diamond tossed his duffle bag at the foot of the steps and admired the peaceful sanctuary he called home. The old Victorian house he was born and raised in was now his. Since purchasing it from his parents after they decided to buy an RV and travel the country, very little had changed. Family photos lined the wide staircase; everything was well used and loved, none of that stuffiness some old houses had. The memories of his childhood played out everywhere he looked.

He'd made it home after months of blood, death, and war that had taken a toll on his body and his spirit. He needed a break, not to mention a week's worth of sleep.

This deployment had been harder than any of the others. Too many of his fellow warriors had been killed. Memories of the bloodshed haunted him every time he closed his eyes. Too many recollections he would have rather left behind. He was a different man than when he left a year ago, and he could no longer look at the world the same way. Everywhere he looked he saw people taking freedom for granted. So many of them didn't even realize that more men and women than he'd care to count gave their lives for those freedoms. This deployment served to remind him just how expensive that freedom was.

Dishes clattered in the kitchen, drawing him from his thoughts and back to the present.

"Wynn?" He made his way toward the large farmhouse kitchen in the rear. Coming around the corner, he expected to find his little sister. Instead, he saw a woman with a short pixie haircut, red hair sticking up every which way, holding a knife in her hand.

"Who are you?" Fear coated her voice.

He looked at the small knife, knowing it would be easy to disarm her if he had to. "Better question is who are you? After all, you're in my house."

"Ace..." Her eyes widened in surprise. "You're not supposed to be here. Wynn said you wouldn't be back for a couple more weeks."

"Well, I'm here, so why don't you tell me who you are?" He leaned against the wide entryway into the kitchen, crossing his arms over his chest.

"Gwen." With a shaky hand, she set the knife on the counter. "Wynn told me I could stay here until I found a place of my own. I came back for my mother's funeral and couldn't leave. You don't realize how much you miss home until you come back."

"Gwyneth London, it can't be." He took in the woman before him. *Wow!*

"You didn't recognize me at first, so I thought maybe you forgot all about me."

"You look so different." Different was an understatement. Her long blonde hair had been replaced with the red spiky do, and she had developed curves in all the right places. She was gorgeous. Gathering himself together, he nodded. "I'm sorry about your mom. She was an amazing woman."

"Thank you." She leaned against the counter. "I was making a sandwich. Can I make you one?"

"No thanks, I grabbed something on my way home from the airport, but go ahead." She turned back to the cutting board and cut into the turkey, tomato, and lettuce sandwich. That was when he saw the slight protruding tummy, the beginnings of the curve of pregnancy. Was she?

"You noticed." Sometime while he was lost in his thoughts she turned around, sandwich in one hand, her other hand resting on the curve of her stomach.

"Are you…?"

"Pregnant? Yes."

"Is that the reason you decided to stay?"

"Let's sit, I'll explain while I eat." She moved past him into the dining room, and took a seat at the head of the long dining table.

She took a bite out of the sandwich before meeting his gaze. "For years I've been so focused on my career, never sparing time for a personal life, let alone dating or even thinking of children."

"Then how?"

"Two years ago I was in a car accident and was in a coma for weeks. When I woke, I realized there was so much more in life. More that I wanted." She ran her hand over her stomach. "Four months ago I decided I wanted to start a family. So I went to a fertility clinic, and well...you can see the results."

"Why not do it the old-fashioned way?" His eyes widened, appalled that she let a doctor impregnate her instead of doing it the way their parents had.

"To do it that way, you need a man. One-night stands tend to get upset when you use them to have a child without telling them. This seemed a better route."

"But you'll be doing it all on your own. No father to help raise the child."

"I can raise a child myself. My mother practically did it with me and I turned out just fine. The important part is there's no father to try to take my child away."

She polished off the rest of her sandwich while he sat there trying to figure out what to say to that. Gwen had never been the average woman. No, she had been strong, and full of life. She'd never let a man or anyone tell her what to do.

"I realize you don't agree..."

"What makes you say that?" He didn't like that she found him so easy to read.

"We might have been out of touch for years, but I know you, Ace Le Diamond. I can see the disappointment in your pretty blue eyes. You were raised in a perfect family by both parents. I wasn't so lucky, and my child won't be either, but she'll never lack for anything. Please don't disrespect my decision just because you don't agree with it."

"Wow." He held up his hands in front of him, warding off her answer. "I said nothing and did nothing to disrespect your decision. I was only thinking back to when we were kids. You always said you wanted a husband, two and a half kids, a dog, and a house with a white picket fence. All these years that I haven't seen you, I just figured you found what you wanted."

He kept it to himself that even though Wynn stayed in touch with her, he deliberately lost touch. The attraction between them had always been strong, drawing them together through everything, but when he joined the military, the distance began, only to worsen when he made the SEAL team. She might have been proud of him, but the fear that lingered in her eyes tore at his heart. Distance seemed to be the only way to avoid it.

He had never wanted to cause her any pain, and seeing it there in her eyes he knew the only way to change it was to step back. To let their friendship drift away until she no longer cared about him. It was hard, and over the years he had thought about her, but giving up his career as a SEAL wasn't an option. He was meant for the excitement and the thrill. It was everything he was.

Marissa Dobson

Born and raised in the Pittsburgh, Pennsylvania area, Marissa Dobson now resides about an hour from Washington, D.C. She's a lady who likes to keep busy, and is always busy doing something. With two different college degrees, she believes you're never done learning.

Being the first daughter to an avid reader, this gave her the advantage of learning to read at a young age. Since learning to read she has always had her nose in a book. It wasn't until she was a teenager that she started writing down the stories she came up with.

Marissa is blessed with a wonderful supportive husband, Thomas. He's her other half and allows her to stay home and pursue her writing. He puts up with all her quirks and listens to her brainstorm in the middle of the night.

Her writing buddies Max (a cocker spaniel) and Dawne (a beagle mix) are always around to listen to her bounce ideas off them. They might not be able to answer, but they are helpful in their own ways.

She love to hear from readers so send her an email at marissa@marissadobson.com or visit her online at http://www.marissadobson.com.

Bearing Secrets: Alaskan Tigers

Other Books by Marissa Dobson

Alaskan Tigers Series:

Tiger Time

The Tiger's Heart

Tigress for Two

Night with a Tiger

Trusting a Tiger

Jinx's Mate

Two for Protection

Bearing Secrets

Stormkin Series:

Storm Queen

Reaper Series:

A Touch of Death

SEALed for You Series:

Ace in the Hole

Explosive Passion

Capturing a Diamond

Fate Series:

Snowy Fate

Sarah's Fate

Mason's Fate

As Fate Would Have It

Half Moon Harbor Resort Series:

Learning to Live

Learning What Love Is

Her Cowboy's Heart

Half Moon Harbor Resort Volume One

Clearwater Series:

Winterbloom

Unexpected Forever

Losing to Win

Christmas Countdown

The Surrogate

Clearwater Romance Volume One

Stand Alone:

Secret Valentine

Restoring Love

The Twelve Seductive Days of Christmas

CPSIA information can be obtained at www.ICGtesting.com
Printed in the USA
LVOW13s2308250614

391664LV00001B/268/P